House of Refuge

By Jamie Lynn Boothe

House of Refuge

Limitless Publishing, LLC
Kailua, HI 96734
www.limitlesspublishing.com

Formatting: Limitless Publishing

ISBN-13: 978-1-64034-947-6

Dedication

I dedicate this novel of inspiration and spirituality and love to one of the best friends I have ever been blessed with in my entire life, Jennifer Butterworth Lyons. She has done more for me than anyone else. Most importantly, she never gave up on me. She never stopped loving me and never stopped believing in me. I love you, Sugarplum.

Chapter One

Trinity

"I've told you over and over I don't want you going! Why will you not listen to me?" Immediately after his harsh words Trinity feels the back of Derrick's hand connect fiercely with her left cheek, knocking her to the ground. "You will not be going!"

She lies motionless and trembling in front of him, scared of what will happen if she upsets him further; the sting throbs on her cheek and fresh tears flow. Her face almost touches the lush carpet and her breathing is rapid. She knows she will have another bruise. It won't be the first time nor the last unless she can find some way out. She knows better than to talk back; it is useless. When he gets angry, he's in control. What he says matters—nothing else.

Derrick, her boyfriend, has been beating her for over a year, but it's gotten worse ever since she started going to church. He does his best to control her, and that's another way of doing so. She slowly and painfully pushes herself up from the floor without arguing and quietly shuffles into the bathroom. When she sees the image of herself in the mirror, she takes deep breaths and shakes her hands to calm herself, willing the tears to stop. She's angry and tired. Tired of getting beat on and sick of living in fear. If she doesn't find some way out of here soon, he will put her in the hospital again, or kill her.

It's Friday. She simply asked Derrick if she could go to church on Sunday. She doesn't think she should have to ask permission, but he controls everything she does. It wasn't always that way. Once upon a time she was madly in love with someone she thought was a good man. She hasn't felt that love in a long time, but fear keeps her bound to him. Fear and the fact she doesn't have any help or a place to go.

She dabs at her quickly swelling lip with a cold washcloth to stop the bleeding and winces. The pain makes her hate him more than ever. Hatred for any living being is something she despises, but she can't help it. Right now, she hates him. She's never understood how someone can hurt the person they are supposed to love. Love doesn't include control and abuse. She stares at herself and shakes her head, wondering for the hundredth time how things ever turned out this way. After a moment she decides to start getting ready because in a couple hours he will want to leave for the bar. She has no desire to go, but doesn't have a choice. She undresses and takes her shower, wishing for the soap and water to wash

2

away the feelings he causes in her, but she knows that isn't possible.

"God…please, help me! I beg you to get me out of the horror I live in. Please!" She whispers quietly beneath the sound of the water. "You are the only One who can help me and I badly need You now." When she's finished, she gets dressed before applying make-up. Derrick doesn't like her wearing too much, but her left eye still has some discoloration from when he hit her last week. He will want that covered so nobody notices. She tries putting mascara on, but her hand trembles.

"Control girl, get control," she whispers to herself as she wills her hand to be still, taking deep breaths and holding back the tears threatening to escape. After a couple of smudges and wiping, she finally succeeds and looks at herself in the mirror. She used to think of herself as an attractive woman. A strong woman of color who had dreams of being a success in the world, a woman with aspirations. But when a person gets beat down enough their hopes begin to dwindle. As she stares at herself she realizes her best features are her green eyes and her smile. That is, when her lips and face aren't bruised, split and bleeding.

Her friends, who are no longer around thanks to Derrick, told her she should be a model. She even considered it once, but fell in love with being the one taking the pictures. She loves being outside and capturing scenes of humanity and nature. She loves to feel the sun on her skin as the wind blows, or the sound as rain pounds the ground and the skies are filled with brilliant lightning. Even those dreams are beginning to fade; her entire life is dying. Sometimes, it feels like it's spiraling downward, out of control.

Apparently she loses track of time because Derrick starts knocking on the door, asking how much longer she will be. He wants to get something to eat before they go to the bar. The hard impact of his fist on the bathroom door causes her to jump and she almost knocks her makeup on the floor.

"I'll be right out," she answers through the door.

"God, please get me through this night. Please, help me, however You may." After another quick prayer she opens the door and walks out to be part of a life she no longer desires.

***

The ride to the bar is uncomfortable as usual, but this time it feels worse. The entire journey she has tingling sensations throughout her body. She doesn't know if it's from dread or from her heart pounding so hard. She's amazed the sound of her heart beating doesn't override the music from the speakers. She doesn't want to talk to him about anything, but he acts as if everything is fine between them. As if he didn't do anything wrong. He won't shut up about needing a few drinks and jamming out to some music. He also says he has some business to take care of, but she doesn't know what he means by that. She has a feeling that whatever it is, she won't like it.

The rain intensifies as they drive into the sparsely lit parking lot. The quarter-size raindrops beat relentlessly onto the blacktop as they ease past other vehicles in search of an empty space close to the door. The sound hitting the roof above them is so loud and rhythmic she has a sort of spiritual feeling God is telling her something, but she pushes the thought to the back of her mind.

At least the sound drowns out some of Derrick's chatter.

When they finally find a parking spot, they reluctantly leave the warm and dry space within the car and hurry through the pouring rain, heads covered with their jackets. They enter the busy club and shake off the excess water. Music is blaring and people appear to be having a good time. They push their way through the crowd to the bar and he orders for them both. He knows she doesn't like to drink, but he buys her a margarita anyway, with no concern for what she wants.

With drinks in hand they watch the crowd on the dance floor and in the surrounding area until a pool table is available. She sips on her bitter-tasting drink and observes the men and women swaying and dancing to the music. She shouldn't call this place a club. It's actually more of a bar with a dance floor and high hopes of business picking up. The owners have tried everything they can. This time they thought adding moving overhead lights and mirrors on the walls for the "clubbing effect" would help. She doesn't like it, but for some reason Derrick does.

They find a small table with chairs near the pool tables. She has to admit that's the only thing she does enjoy doing with Derrick—playing pool. She is better than him but has to downplay most of the time, purposely missing easy shots. She knows what will happen when they get home if he doesn't win almost all the games, especially if he has too much to drink. The games he'll want to play then will consist of either beating her or rough sex; usually both. She prefers losing at pool than losing a tooth.

By the time they play three games he is already starting on his third beer. It is going to be a long night; in her head, she is trying to think of a way to get away, to run from him forever. Halfway through the fourth game, two of his friends saunter in and make their way over. When she sees them she has a good idea what he means by "business." She ignores them as they talk because she knows they are drug dealers and doesn't want anything to do with them or their "business."

She sits at the table, the game forgotten, and looks at her drink, wishing she could buy herself a soda or ginger ale. What she sees next she can't believe. In front of everyone, Derrick hands one of his friends a wad of money and receives something in return. She doesn't know exactly what it is, but she is sure it's a drug of some type. Probably marijuana, which she despises.

She's had enough of this life. She has to find some way out. She watches the crowd and searches her fearful brain for an idea, any idea. If the opportunity shows itself she will run in an instant. She will turn tail, go somewhere and forget about everything she has in Torrington, Connecticut. It's all material things and can be replaced. She has no family here and the life she has isn't worth living.

She remembers her prayer in the bathroom at home and hopes what she asked for will be very soon. Her prayer is answered a lot sooner than she anticipates.

Derrick steps away from his two friends over to where she's sitting and yells over the music. "Are you having a good time, babe?" She knows she has to lie so she nods. "Good." His eyes turn serious. "I have something to do, but I won't be long. Stay right here."

She watches him walk over and talk to the bartender and his two friends disappear into the crowd. She has no clue what he is talking to the guy about, but she sees the bartender look around then lets him into the office behind the bar. Her heart suddenly begins beating furiously; she feels God pulling on her. She knows right then that she is going to do the unimaginable. She can't believe it's happening so fast; she doesn't have a plan or a place to go nor does she have her car, but she can't take it any longer. She feels an overwhelming urge to take action immediately so she's going to run for it. She knows what the consequences will be if he catches her, but she doesn't care anymore. She's out of there.

Frantically, she grabs her jacket and weaves her way through the crowd. With each step, someone seems to squash her and bump into her. Her mind starts yelling that she won't make it in time, but she doesn't slow or stop. She can feel something or someone pulling on her heart and soul, telling her to keep putting one foot in front of the other. When she finally reaches the door she rushes through it, out into the storm. With the skies covered with

7

clouds and only a few overhead lamps in the lot, there isn't much light. The rain hasn't eased but she doesn't allow that to keep her beneath the awning.

She rushes out into the night without a clue where to go. The rain soaks through instantly as she looks for some place to hide. Without time to think, she runs from car to car trying to find one unlocked. She tries one last car before giving up hope. The back door opens, she falls into it, and slams the door behind her. Seconds later she can hear someone screaming her name. Someone who is filled with anger and hatred and wants to hurt her.

***

Derrick

In the office behind the bar Derrick looks at what lies in front of him. "So this is the best you have?" Derrick asks. It's the first time he's met this supplier, but rumor is he's the man to get stuff from.

"It's the best that can be got," the man replies.

"How much for an ounce?" he asks as he holds the bag of white powder gently in his palm.

"One thousand dollars and that's a steal. I want your business so I'm giving you a first time buyer's special."

Scratching the stubble on his chin, Derrick thinks it over for a moment and decides to go ahead and make the buy. If he isn't happy with the sales, he can always find someone else next time; he's always good about finding connections. He knows he will make a decent profit on the streets and from a few guys at work so he isn't too worried. He hands the man cash, deposits the bag in the inside pocket of his jacket, and looks at the clock on the wall. Five minutes is how long he's been in there. He doesn't like leaving Trinity alone for very long—he never knows who might be hitting on his property.

"I'll get back to you when I need more." Derrick walks back out to the loud music and lights. Trinity isn't sitting where she was told to stay and his temper flares. He walks toward their table and searches the room as he goes. He isn't happy and has a bad feeling, but gives her the benefit of the doubt; she may be in the restroom. He waits a few minutes, then checks the restrooms, waiting for someone to either come out or go in so he can check on Trinity. Derrick catches a gorgeous brunette on her way out and describes Trinity, but the woman says there isn't anyone else in there. The sounds of the crowd and music that earlier were too loud are no longer of any interest to him. With clenched fists and boiling blood he runs outside, into the rain, searching for her. He screams her name as he runs around the parking lot, getting soaking wet. If he gets his hands on her, she will never forget the beating to come when they get home.

Chapter Two

Trinity

The fear running through Trinity's veins as she hides in a stranger's car is the most powerful force she has ever experienced.

Powerful is an understatement. What she's doing is the unthinkable, something she never thought she would have the courage to do. If he finds her she is as good as dead. Listening to the rain beating down on the roof of the car, Trinity feels like she's inside a thin tin can, like a sardine in one of the small containers her father used to enjoy eating. Trembling and quiet as a mouse she can still hear Derrick screaming her name, getting too close for comfort as he searches the parking lot. Thankfully, the lighting in the parking lot is dismal and she fled a few minutes before he had any chance to know she was gone. She can't believe how fortunate she is to have found an unlocked car. She hopes whoever owns it doesn't return anytime soon.

Trinity does her best to be quiet as she shivers and lies on the floor of the car. She's soaking wet from head to toe and beginning to get a cramp in her side from how she is positioned. She's scared for her life and doesn't realize it's highly unlikely he will hear her teeth chattering.

She feels around behind her in search of something to cover herself with as she lies on the back floorboard. She finds a blanket and pulls it over herself, but it barely conceals her. She is sure it has only been minutes since she got inside the car, but it feels like hours. Finally she doesn't hear Derrick screaming anymore. Maybe he accepted that she somehow got away. She has no doubt he is furious. She knows if he gets his hands on her he will be more than happy to show her how angry he is.

Suddenly, the tight space is filled with light and she feels like her heart will explode from her chest. She expects to be drug back out into the rain by her feet, beaten and cursed at, but nothing happens other than the door slamming shut. Seconds later she feels the car move forward and holds her breath as they move slowly through the rain. She can only guess what will happen next. Is the person driving a man or a woman? Will they notice her on the floorboard, and if they do, how will they react when they find her? She starts praying harder than ever before then hears a woman's voice from the front seat, almost sending her into shock.

"It's okay, you are safe now. I know you are scared, but I will not hurt you. You can sit up."

Trinity doesn't know what to think or say. A

11

whimper threatens to escape and her heart hammers against her chest hard enough to be painful. Slowly, she pushes herself up from the floor and as her whole body trembles, she sits on the edge of the seat, wrapping the blanket around her. Drops of water from her hair run into her eyes. Wiping them away, she sees an older lady driving. From the backseat she looks into the rearview mirror and sees the woman's soft, compassionate eyes.

"What's your name, dear?" the lady asks as she glances back and captures her gaze. "Trinity," she barely whispers.

"That's a beautiful name and whether you know it or not, it's religious and stands for something. My name is Mattie. I saw what was going on and when I saw you hide, I knew I had to help you. Like I said, you are safe now."

Stunned by the stranger's compassion and generosity, she asks with a trembling voice,

"How did you see me?"

"I was in the business next to the bar and I happened to glance out the window because it was raining so terribly hard. I guess it was perfect timing when I saw you get in the car. Almost as soon as you slammed the door I could hear that man screaming for you. I didn't have to be a genius to realize you were in danger."

Trinity doesn't say anything at first. Her emotions are roiling inside of her and she's struggling to keep them at bay. She watches the rain slide diagonally down the windows and listens to it beat upon the outside of the car. She feels lost and hopeless, more than she ever has in her life, but at least she's not with Derrick. She remembers how her life used to be. It feels like another dimension and she wants it back.

She hates how her life turned out since she's been with Derrick. The past year has been the worst, and now she is in a stranger's car with no clue where they are going or what will happen next. All she knows is she has to rely on God more than ever. He is truly all she has left. The problem is she doesn't know if God will help her. She doesn't feel she deserves His help. Then again, she realizes, if it wasn't for God she wouldn't have been able to get away or find a safe car to hide in.

"Where are we going?" Trinity asks a little louder than before.

"Is there someplace you can go? If not I will take you to my house. My husband is there and like me, he will be more than happy to help. He's a pastor."

"I have nowhere I can go," Trinity replies as she slides back against the seat feeling defeated. "Thank you for helping me."

The rest of the drive is silent, except for the rain that relentlessly continues its downpour.

Tears begin to escape and mix with the water dripping from Trinity's soaking wet hair. A pastor?

She can feel God working just like the saying goes—He works in mysterious ways. Believing God is with her helps her feel safe. After a few more minutes they pull into the driveway of Mattie's house.

"We're here." Mattie turns to look at her and says, "I know you don't know me or my husband, but I promise that you have nothing to be afraid of.

13

Come with me."

Mattie gets out of the car and Trinity follows behind her, running as quickly as they can to get out of the dreadful weather. Once inside Mattie calls out that she's home and has brought a guest. Trinity stands on the doormat, unsure what to do next as large drops of water fall from her onto the polished floor. Before she can think anything of it, Trinity is looking at an older man with balding hair and a plump build. He resembles her grandfather except for the fact he's white. He has a kind and compassionate look about him, and she feels at ease with them both. "Well now, who may you be, young lady?"

"Trinity. I'm sorry to be causing you any trouble," she answers and lowers her gaze.

"Oh dear—you are no trouble," Mattie assures her. "Come with me so we can find you a change of clothes. You are soaking wet and will surely catch pneumonia."

Trinity tries to smile as she follows Mattie down the hall. They walk into a small bedroom that obviously isn't theirs. The bed appears unused and there isn't much sitting on the furniture as far as pictures and knickknacks.

"This is the spare bedroom. We don't normally have many guests, but once in a while we do help someone in need so that's what we use it for," Mattie tells her as she begins to rummage through the closet. "Okay, here we go. It ain't much but the last woman we helped left it behind and it looks like it might fit you."

Trinity looks at the sweatsuit that Mattie hands

her. It looks relatively new and she holds it in her hands and enjoys how comfortable and warm the fabric feels.

"Thank you, I really appreciate this," she says, her head hanging low.

Placing her hand on Trinity's arm, Mattie says, "It's no problem. The bathroom is down the hall on your right. Just come into the kitchen when you are finished. I believe Howard was preparing something for dinner so if you are hungry, you are more than welcome to join us."

"Thank you."

Trinity walks into the bathroom, closes the door, and stares at her image in the mirror. What she sees staring back is frightening, and she hopes she will never have to see herself this way again. Her eyes are bloodshot with dark bags beneath them, her bottom lip is swollen from where Derrick hit her, and her hair is all over the place. Closing her eyes, she fights to not break into tears. Her bottom lip quivers and she grips the edge of the sink until her knuckles turn white.

Shaking her head, she can't believe the mess she's in. For so long, in every aspect of her life, she worked hard to be happy. Being a twenty-nine year old woman with no children she had, until recently, a decent career in photography for a blossoming magazine. She eats healthy and knows she's an attractive black woman.

She was happy until just over a year ago when she made the mistake of moving in with boyfriend. She was in love and thought he loved her. Everything had been so great between them,

15

but almost as soon as she moved in he changed, dramatically. He started showing a side of himself she had never seen before and it didn't take long until he began hitting her. Lately it had gotten much worse; she had grown afraid for her life. She knew she had to somehow escape his torment. Now she's in a house with two people she's never met before but who are willing to help her. They seem nice, but she's scared. She hasn't any idea of what's going to happen and that terrifies her.

Opening her eyes, she lets them fall on her reflection again and remembers her mother's reaction when Trinity told her she had fallen for a white man. Her momma was the old-fashioned type and at first she wasn't happy about it, but Derrick fooled her too. Not long after she met him her momma passed away from a heart-attack. She misses her more than ever, but in a way it's good that she doesn't know what has happened since.

Shaking her head, she undresses, cleans up the best she can and gets dressed in the sweatsuit. After taking another look at herself, she nervously walks into the kitchen where Mattie and Howard are setting the table for three. They both look up and smile at her.

"Perfect timing," Howard tells her. "Supper's ready. Are you hungry?"

Trinity nods her head. "Yeah, a little, thank you."

They sit around a small oak table and Howard and Mattie reach for her hands to say grace. Even though she wants to get closer to God and get in church, this is something she isn't accustomed to.

Saying a prayer before a meal was unheard of in Derrick's house. It feels good and she holds their hands, closes her eyes, and listens as Howard prays over the food.

"Lord, our Father and Savior, I thank You tonight for the blessings You continue to place in our lives. I thank You for the opportunities and the guidance to help us on our way. Thank You Lord for blessing our table with this food and I ask that it will suffice our needs. Most importantly, Lord, I thank You for gracing our home with Trinity tonight. I ask that You help us be able to help her if she will give us the honor, and whatever is in Your plan for her that You give her the strength, courage, guidance, comfort, and acceptance she will need to walk through it safely. In Your name I pray, Amen."

When Howard finishes, they begin to fill their plates and she sits watching, suddenly uncomfortable.

"Help yourself dear, there's more than enough. When Howard cooks, and thankfully it's most of the time, he usually makes enough for a small army."

"It's a good thing you love my cooking," he jokes.

"I do, but what I love most is me not having to cook most of the time."

Trinity can't help but giggle at the two of them. She has only been there about thirty minutes, but already finds them not only sincere, but cute together. It's obvious each one adores the other. There isn't a lot of talk during supper and afterward she is told to sit when she tries to help clean up the dishes. When the dishwasher is filled and running, they all go into the living room and she knows it's time to tell them more about herself and her situation.

"So Trinity, I hope you don't mind, but I think you'll agree that maybe we should know a little about what is going on. Please, don't be afraid, and we will never judge you by anything you tell us. We only want to help and knowing what is going on will help us help you," Howard kindly says to her. She knows he's right and she isn't surprised by him asking, but that doesn't make it easier. She'd rather not talk about it, but they have the right to know. She takes a deep breath and starts twirling a strand of her hair with her fingers. Looking at them, she begins to tell her story.

"I don't know exactly where to start, so I guess I'll tell you a little about me first. I'm originally from North Carolina. That's where I was born, but when I was five my mother took me to Colorado when my father passed. We lived in Boulder the entire time until I chose to move here to Connecticut to pursue a career in photography. I didn't make a lot of friends because I have always had a hard time with that, plus I was so busy building a life here. Not too long after I moved I met a guy named Derrick. It took a while, but he finally talked me into going out with him; he was a smooth talker. I didn't know it then, of course, and I fell in love with him. We dated about a year and I truly believed he was the one. Momma was still in Colorado and her health was starting to get bad.

When I told her about Derrick, she wasn't real happy about me dating a white man. She worried about me too much. So I talked him into going out there to meet her and like I said, he was a smooth talker and he managed to convince her he's a great guy. Shortly after we came home I moved in with him. That was when things started to change and not in a good way. He started yelling at me over little things. I thought it was because he was getting stressed over money and work. I didn't want to think he was a bad guy. I was still in love so I did my best to not worry about it too much. Then he wanted to know everything I was doing. Where I was at all times and who I was with. It became really stressful on me. Then one night I wasn't feeling good and he had been drinking too much and wanted to have sex, but I didn't want to. To him, my feelings didn't matter. He hit me, almost knocked me unconscious, and raped me. It's escalated ever since."

She stops for a moment to breathe and get control of her nerves, hoping she won't start crying. Her hands are shaking. Howard and Mattie watch her with compassion and don't say a word.

"Well, what happened tonight is I asked him if I could start going to church again. It infuriated him. He hates the idea of me being in church. He yelled at me and busted my lip, knocking me to the floor. I didn't fight back. Instead, I went to the bathroom and got ready to go to the bar that he insisted on making me go to with him. I knew he would want to have sex when we got home, but it sickened me to even think about being touched by him again. I should mention, too, that not long ago I found out he was dealing drugs. That was partly why he wanted to go and I despise that he does that. When he went in the office at the bar to buy what he wanted I knew it could be the only chance I would have to run and I didn't hesitate. That was when I hid in your car."

A moment passes before Mattie speaks. "When you left him tonight, you left everything else behind as well, didn't you?"

Trinity nods as a tear manages to escape. "I had no choice. I had no time to plan, so...yes. I have nothing right now."

Howard is silent until Mattie asks if she was afraid for her life and she nods her head in silence. She isn't able to say anymore because of the lump in her throat.

"I know it may not look like it right now," he says, "but there is a light at the end of the tunnel. This isn't the first time we have had a young woman in need of help placed in our lives. God placed you with us to keep you safe, even if it's for a short while. We have a very trusted friend who I know will be helpful if you want me to call him."

A tear falls onto the carpet and Trinity wipes her eyes with the back of her hand. Mattie hands her a box of tissues and she blows her nose. She tries to say something, but her heart says otherwise. She breaks down into uncontrollable sobs and she folds into herself. Mattie sits beside her and holds her like she was her own child, comforting her. Howard sits with his eyes closed and quietly says a prayer. Once she is calm enough to talk again, she asks who his friend is and how he can help.

"His name is Gates, and he used to live near us. He is a Marine veteran and was a Navy Seal before he decided to have a more private life and moved here. Now he lives in Virginia in a small town called Moneta, near a lake he speaks highly of. We actually talk about once or twice a month. We stay in touch not only because he became like a son to us, but because he has helped someone else like you before. We trust him with our lives if it ever comes down to that."

"No offense to either of you, but right now I'm not sure if I can completely trust anyone."

"I understand, but what other choices do you have?" Howard asks.

Trinity feels defeated and hangs her head. "None."

"Do you want me to call him and see if he will help?" Howard asks.

Trinity thinks for a moment and knows she really doesn't have any other options. She has to get away. She can't stay here and put them in danger as well. If Derrick finds her she is as good as dead. She truly believes that. She nods her head and whispers "Yes."

"Okay, I'll call him right away. Why don't you try to get some rest and we'll talk more tomorrow. Mattie will help you get comfortable. Everything will be okay. Have faith and trust God."

Howard makes the phone call to his friend and Trinity walks with Mattie to the spare room, feeling like the world has been laid upon her shoulders. Mattie talks to her for only a moment and lets her know if she needs anything through the night to not hesitate to ask. She says "Good night" and closes the door, leaving Trinity alone.

She gets beneath the covers and cries herself to sleep, but sleep is fitful. She tosses and turns through the night as she battles with nightmares. Several times she wakes up sweating and wanting to run, but she has nowhere to go. The last thought before sleep finally comforts her is what will happen to her? Will she ever find peace again, or will her future be filled with more torture?

Chapter Three

Trinity

Trinity lies on her stomach and slowly begins to wake. Her eyes crack open when she feels a slight pain in her neck and a moan escapes. Darkness still dominates the room and she realizes it's still very early. She thinks about how weird it feels to wake up in a place she has never been. She has no clue what time it is, but she can still hear the rain and wonders if it will stop any time soon. She hopes so because the dreariness makes her feel worse. She thinks about what's happened and where it has brought her.

She turns on her side and squeezes the soft pillow beneath her. She wishes with all her might that she could somehow go back in time before she ever met Derrick, knowing what she has learned, so when she does meet him she will know better. She knows it's a waste of time thinking that way, though. She can't do anything about what has happened.

23

She closes her eyes, hoping sleep will comfort her again, but as time passes she accepts rest has forsaken her and emerges from the comfort of the bed. As she softly shuffles down the hall and into the living room, her eyes become better focused in the dimly lit house. Standing near the kitchen, she can see the clock on the cablebox reads barely six o'clock. She is a guest in Mattie and Howard's home and isn't comfortable with touching anything so she sits on the couch, looking through the newspaper. She has nothing else to do. Before long her eyes grow heavy. She is almost ready to go back to bed when she hears a door open.

"Good morning dear, are you okay?" Mattie softly asks her.

Trinity nods. "Yes ma'am. I wasn't sleeping well so I got up a little while ago. I didn't wake you, did I?"

"Oh no, you were quiet as a mouse. I always get up around this time whether I want to or not. It's my inner clock I guess. Do you want some coffee?"

"Yes, please. I thought about making some, but I didn't want to make any noise and I didn't feel comfortable going through your cabinets."

"Oh phew, come in the kitchen with me to keep me company. Howard will sleep for about another hour so we can have a little girl talk."

"Sounds good to me."

The aroma of the brewing coffee fills the kitchen and they sit at the table. Mattie asks, "So you said last night that you are originally from North Carolina. What part?"

"Asheboro."

"What is that near?"

"It's only about a thirty minute drive from Greensboro. Have you ever heard of that?"

"Yes, I've heard of Greensboro, but I haven't ever been down there. Is it nice?"

"Well, I like it down there. It's my home, and there are a lot of small towns around. The people are more laid back than up here. The winters aren't usually as rough and the cost of living is cheaper. What I miss the most, though, about North Carolina is its beauty. And Asheboro is only a three hour or so drive from Myrtle Beach in South Carolina. I love that beach."

"Maybe you'll get to go home soon. You never know what God has planned for you."

The gurgling sound of the coffeemaker interrupts them and they both make a steaming cup. They sit back down and don't say anything else at first. Trinity wants to ask her a few things about faith and church but is nervous. Instead, she asks about the friend who might help her. "He's a very nice young man once you get to know him. When you first meet him he may come across as quiet and reserved, but that's only because he has to get a feel for you, so to speak. Once he decides you are okay you won't be able to shut him up."

Trinity laughs and is surprised at how good it feels. "So you were able to get hold of him last night then?"

"I'm not sure if Howard did or not, to be honest. I know he called him and left a message, but I went to bed soon after you did. I'm sure he will tell us when he gets up."

They continue chatting about nothing in particular, enjoying a relaxing conversation. Mattie tells her about what it's like to be a preacher's wife—the joys and hardships of it. They just finish their first cup of coffee when seconds later Howard walks into the kitchen. Mattie kisses him good morning, then pours him a cup as he greets them.

"How did you sleep, Trinity? I wasn't expecting to see you up before me."

"Not very well, I'm afraid. Being in a strange place and with everything I have on my plate I didn't think I would."

"You can go back to bed if you want, or maybe a nap later. It's Saturday and with all this rain there isn't much else to do today. Of course you may want to get ready for your trip. Mentally at least. It will be a long ride for you both."

"Oh, so you talked to your friend then?"

He takes a long sip of coffee, the steam from his cup fogging his glasses. Removing them, Howard nods and answers, "Yes, I did, and I took the liberty to tell him what you told us last night. Most of it, not the real personal things. That wasn't my place. I only told him what he needed to know."

"And he wants to help me even though he's never met me?"

"He does, and he should be here around four or five. He's actually not too far from here. He happens to be visiting someone and said he will come here to get you before he goes back to Virginia."

Her eyes fall to her cup and fear begins to ease back into her mind. She has mixed emotions about leaving with a man she's never met, even if Mattie and Howard trust him.

"I know you only met us last night, and after so much drama in your life. You have no idea what your future holds and you've never met Gates, but God didn't put you into our hands for nothing. We trust Gates with our lives, if that means anything to you. You have nothing to be afraid of," Mattie assures her.

"I know and I will do my best. I'm sorry I'm not in the same place as you both are with God. I guess I need to be though," Trinity replies, and hesitates. With a mixture of emotions written on her face she continues. "I want to. I want to know God, I really do. I want to get back to church, but for some reason I'm scared. I don't know why. Maybe, when things cool down a little, I will start going again in Virginia. I hope so, at least."

"God is the One who will never let you down," Howard replies with a certain touch of sensitivity and compassion in his voice. Trinity looks at him and smiles.

"Why don't I make some pancakes and bacon?" Mattie offers.

Everyone agrees breakfast sounds good, and nothing more is mentioned about Trinity's situation. Instead the talk turns to several other topics, which include thoughts of getting a dog, the weather, and more about Trinity's childhood home. The change of conversation and breakfast help her feel better. She helps clean up then lies back down for a nap. She hopes to get at least a couple hours of sleep before Howard and Mattie's friend arrives. She highly doubts she will be comfortable enough to sleep on the drive to Virginia.

***

Trinity sleeps longer than she means to and when she wakes, she hears a new voice coming from the living room. Her heart begins to pound and her nerves betray her. She doesn't think she slept the whole day away. Can their friend already be here? She takes a deep breath and starts to go see, but hesitates. Standing at the doorway of the spare bedroom, she fidgets and shakes her hands, trying to calm down. She doesn't want to be a basket-case in front of them. Finally, after a few minutes of steady breathing and pacing around the room she opens the door and walks out. Mattie and Howard welcome her with smiles, and a man who she assumes is their friend, Gates, looks at her with interest. He is an attractive man. She imagined him to be bigger, tougher looking, and with some visible tattoos, but he still looks as if he can probably handle himself.

"Hey Trinity, I would like you to meet my friend Gates. As it turns out he was able to get here a few hours early," Howard tells her.

She smiles nervously at Gates and nods. "Hi."

"Hey, it's nice to meet you."

"Nice to meet you, too. Forgive me if I seem a little out of it. I'm a little overwhelmed."

"You don't have to explain or apologize. I understand and I'm sure Howard and Mattie told you about me."

"They did last night, yes. A little."

28

"Okay, good. I'm sorry to rush you but we need to go very soon. It's a long drive and from the weather report, it's going to be raining the majority of the way back home."

She's caught off-guard by having to leave so fast, but she doesn't have anything with her so she is ready to go.

"Uhhh, sure, whatever you say."

His eyes glitter and she notices they are a bright green. Almost hypnotizing. Mattie offers to make sandwiches to take with them but Gates says a cup of coffee for them both will be fine.

"If that's okay with you?" he asks Trinity. "We'll stop on the way somewhere and get a bite to eat if you get hungry."

"Yeah, that's fine," she says back, but is irritated that he isn't a little more considerate, whether she wants a sandwich or not.

She looks at Howard and Mattie and feels gratitude toward them. She doesn't know what to say, but feels she should hug and thank them both. They hug her back and ask her to please keep in touch when she can.

"I will, I promise. I should get changed before I leave so you can have these clothes back."

"No, don't worry about those things. You'll need them more than I will," Mattie replies and kisses Trinity on her cheek. "We will be praying for you."

Gates takes the two cups of coffee and says it's time to go. She hugs Mattie and Howard goodbye again and feels horrible, thinking it may be the last time she'll ever see them. She can't explain it, but she feels she should pray for them as well. When she looks out of the windshield of Gates' Jeep through the rain at them, a lump fills her throat. She tells herself she can do this. What choice does she have?

***

She watches the trees as Gates drives by at seventy miles an hour; they are a blur through the passenger side window. He hasn't said more than a few words and she has no idea what to talk about. The silence is deafening and she hopes it won't be like this the entire way to Virginia, or it will be a very long ride. They have been on the road for at least an hour and she needs to use the bathroom, but is nervous about saying anything. She decides feeling that way is ridiculous. She takes a deep breath for courage and spurts it out.

"Yeah, that's no problem. I was thinking the same thing. I need to get some gas anyhow," he replies.

I like his voice. She goes back to staring out the window and watching the rain until they get to a gas station. She assumes he is from Connecticut from what Howard told her, but she isn't sure. Howard mentioned Gates lives in Virginia now, so his accent is hard to place. She'll ask soon enough when they are more comfortable with each other. She has no plans on getting too comfortable, though. The idea of even being alone with a strange man is unsettling after what she's been through, but she doesn't have a lot of choices at the moment. Where else can she turn?

Gates

Gates pumps the gas as Trinity walks into the store to use the restroom. He knows only what his friends told him about her and he is okay with that for now. He helped one other girl in the past and didn't think it would happen again, but there she is, smack dab in the middle of his life. She is so quiet, and by the looks of her he has a feeling she will be the sensitive type. He understands she's nervous. Probably scared from whatever she's been through. He admits that even though she's roughed up a little and could use a change of clothes, beneath all of that is a beautiful woman. A woman like her, in the past before his tour of duty, would have made him a very happy man, but that is something he can't think about. He has to help her, not lust after her. He walks inside and buys them both another cup of coffee and a snack.

"This is just to hold us over until we get closer to Virginia," Gates says when he hands her the food and coffee.

"That's fine."

"We'll stop to eat at a place I've been to on occasion."

"That's fine, too."

When they get back on the interstate, Trinity speaks up again. "Can we listen to some music? I don't really care what it is; just something to break up the silence."

Gates leans forward and presses a button to turn

31

the radio on. "Sure, go ahead and find whatever you want. I don't have any preferences either."

After dozens of miles, he notices Trinity has fallen asleep. At least it appears so. *It's for the best.* He knows she will need all the rest she can get, especially once she starts working on the schedule he plans for her.

The rain becomes even more of a downpour, forcing him to drive slower than he'd hoped. The last thing he wants is to get into an accident on the way home with Trinity in the car.

Thankfully, there isn't a lot of traffic right now. He focuses on the road, keeping the car between the lines, but occasionally glances at her as she sleeps. He remembers the other woman he helped a couple of years earlier, Katherine, and the mess she had been in. He shakes his head in memory. Even though he saw some horrible things while he was a Seal, he is still amazed at how cruel some men are. He remembers growing up with a single mother. She was one of the most incredible women he ever knew. As the time passes and Gates handles the car through the rain toward Virginia, he thinks about his mother and how the years without her since she passed have been hard for him.

A single mother raising only him, she rarely mentioned dating or doing anything frivolous. She worked hard trying to make ends meet and have the very best life for the both of them. Then right after he graduated high school, she went to her doctor for her normal checkup. He recalls her telling him the doctor wanted to run some blood tests; those results led her to have a mammogram. The results brought the worst news possible and even though she fought it like a champ, the cancer took her from him quicker than expected. She was and always would be the best person he ever had in his life.

Before his emotions can get the best of him he shakes his head, wipes his eyes, and focuses harder on the road. Trinity begins snoring beside him and he grins. A day will come that he will use that against her—in fun, of course. He knows she has been through hard times, but hopefully they will get along fine. If things go well enough they will connect and be friends like he is with Katherine.

Chapter Four

Trinity

Trinity sits on the back deck and stares out at the sparkling lake, watching the early morning sun spread its warm light on the calm water. She's thankful it finally stopped raining. She is sick of hearing it and seeing it. It's early and she enjoys the silence. Gates is inside doing whatever it is he usually does in the mornings. He seems to be consumed by something. They saw each other in passing as they both got their coffee, still not at ease with regular conversation. When she walked into the kitchen earlier she almost bumped into him as he was walking out. Again, a few minutes later it seemed she was getting in his way. To avoid him she stepped outside with her cup. She has a lot of questions, but doesn't know how to begin. She's sure he's curious about her as well.

Over the rim of her cup she watches a squirrel

run across the grass, another one right behind it. Her heart feels good seeing them play and chase one another. She watches them zig zag around then up one of the trees until she loses sight of them. Her eyes dart around the yard in search of any other small creatures. She has always been a country girl at heart, and being among nature calms her soul. She can't help but to feel more at peace, and smiles. Leaving her hometown when she was a child is one thing she wishes she never had to do, but she didn't have a say in it. If it had been up to her she would have grown up in the country.

She had a good life in Boulder growing up, but it still wasn't as grand as being among the nature of Virginia or the Carolinas. So many things happened, mostly good, and she was excited about her blossoming career until her life in Connecticut with Derrick changed. At the time, she believed things were right for her, and they probably would have been if it hadn't been for him. Then again, she knows the same thing could have happened in North Carolina. Sometimes she feels like some of it was her fault. Just like the old saying goes, hindsight is twenty/twenty.

In the small town of Moneta, she thinks maybe, just maybe, things are beginning to look up. She has to try and have faith and see what happens. She has to learn to live in the moment, and do what is necessary to make her life better. It's still too early to tell what might happen, and thinking about the possibilities makes her heart hammer against her chest.

A slight breeze caresses her skin and she can

smell the fragrance of honeysuckles. God knows she missed being surrounded by nature. She thinks about last night when she and Gates arrived at his cabin. It was late and they were both tired so neither stayed up to talk. Gates showed her around and said they would talk in the morning. Surprisingly, she slept better than the night before, probably because she was so tired from the ride. Even though he showed her the cabin last night, it is big so she wants to walk around later to get a better feel for the place where she will be living for…who knows how long.

"Good morning."

Caught off guard, Trinity almost drops her cup and spills some of her coffee in her lap. She turns and sees Gates standing in the doorway behind the screen door. "Good morning," she replies, trying not to sound flustered.

"Sorry, I didn't mean to startle you. How did you sleep?"

"It's okay, I was lost in my thoughts. Better than I did the night before, thank you. Did you sleep well?"

He smiles in reply. "Not too shabby, thank you."

He doesn't say anything else as he looks out over the still damp grass. She tries to think of something to ask him as she watches him take in the view, and wonders what's going through his mind. In front of her, right now, he is a mystery to her, as she is to him.

"So, have you been living in this cabin for a long time? It's beautiful here."

Gates sits in the chair next to her and answers.

"I've owned this place for a few years. I love it here. I have found some serenity since I've been here. Having the privilege of waking up every morning to that view in front of us helps me a lot. Seeing squirrels and sometimes watching deer walk around makes me feel more grounded. I don't plan on leaving this place for a very long time."

She quietly nods and fully understands what he means by being grounded with nature. There's a sort of connection if one allows it to be. Breathing in the fresh air and the fragrance of nature is already helping her.

Holding her cup with both hands, she looks at him with a ton of curiosity. She wants to know who this man truly is, what makes him tick, but she feels it'll take some time to get that out of him. He doesn't seem like the kind of man to just throw it all out on the table at once.

"I know what you mean about the connection part, and I can see how it can bring peace to your life, that's for sure," she replies. "I think if I could live somewhere like this all the time I wouldn't have as much stress. At least I would hope not."

He looks at her and says, "I wouldn't be anywhere else," then pauses. "I know you probably have a million things going through your mind and you want to know about me and what will happen from here on out. I know I would if I were in your shoes. Today, we will rest and you can walk around to get a good idea and feel for the place. You will be here for a while unless you choose to leave. You are not being held here against your will. In about an hour I'll fix some breakfast then we'll sit and have a long talk. I have to run to the store first, but I'm as curious about you as you are about me."

She looks at him and wonders if he is able to read her mind. Smiling, she says, "Okay, that sounds like a good idea. I would like to take a shower while you are gone, but I don't have any clothes other than what I have on and what I wore the other night, and they need to be washed. I don't have any underwear either."

He nods and purses his lips in understanding. "I'm sorry; I'm glad you told me, I wasn't thinking about that." He rubs his temples. "I guess there's a change in plans then. I will have to take you to Bedford to go to Walmart so you can get some clothes and whatever else you may need. You shouldn't have to wait on things like that. We can get some breakfast while we are out."

"Just let me know when you are ready."

"Half an hour," he tells her. "I need my coffee first."

She agrees and sits back, thinking about the upcoming discussion. Will he be open with her? How much detail will he give about himself? What will she be willing to tell him? If nothing else, the conversation will certainly be interesting.

***

They are more talkative on the ride to Bedford, and Gates asks how she ended up in this situation. He already knows some details provided by Mattie and Howard, but he wants to hear the story from Trinity. She tells him about her boyfriend, Derrick, how they met, and how things started out great. She fills in the story with his controlling behavior which led to him hitting her.

She finishes with the last night she saw Derrick, and how she was suddenly thrust into their mutual friends' lives.

When Trinity stops speaking, there is an air of silence and she stares out at the landscape. After a moment, he breaks the silence by telling her about himself.

"I'm originally from Roanoke, which isn't far from here. When I was five years old, my parents moved to Moneta, but it was a lot different than it is now. The lake is man-made, so it wasn't as beautiful then as it is now, plus the state park wasn't around at the time. To keep a long story short, living in the country was a good thing for me because it helped me escape the horrors of growing up. My father was an alcoholic and my stepmother was abusive. I ran out into the woods and to a creek to fish as often as I could. I graduated high school and went into the Marine Corps less than a week later. It was the best way out of my life. When I joined the Corps, I was angry at life and needed adventure. I wanted to travel and the Marines helped me do that. I didn't have a close family life, or anything else, that was healthy for me. Later, a friend talked me into joining the Navy Seals. That was the toughest year of my life, but I was stubborn enough to force my way through it. As a Seal, I was in dangerous situations and experienced things I wouldn't wish on anyone. I still have nightmares once in a while, but not as bad as they used to be. I lived in Connecticut at one point; that's how I met Howard and Mattie. I still don't know why, exactly, but we grew close, fast. Eventually I moved back here and bought the cabin not too long after I got out. I wanted and seriously needed to be alone for a while. I needed the peace and quiet, the view, and watching the animals to help bring me back to life. It was as close as I could get to solitude without being a hermit."

"I'm sorry to hear that," Trinity whispers, and genuinely means it.

"Thanks."

"With what you were doing in the military I guess you never married."

"No, it wasn't the right time, plus I wasn't ready for something serious. I'm not proud of it, but I guess you could say when I had the chance, I was a little wild. I wouldn't have been a good husband, or boyfriend for that matter."

"How long have you been out?"

"A little over seven years."

"So that makes us about the same age."

"Yeah, I suppose it does."

"What kind of work do you do now?" She continues with the questions.

He takes a breath and glances at her, before answering. She starts to feel bad about bombarding him. "I have chosen not to work a full-time job. I hate the thought of being told what to do by anyone since I've gotten out. I've done a lot of side jobs that have paid well, and I'm actually a pretty handy guy to have around to fix things. I stay busy for the most part, plus I have money saved. I'm thinking about starting my own handyman business. Maybe next spring. Winter will be here soon so I'll probably wait until after that."

They arrive at Walmart before she can ask him anything else. She wants to finish the conversation later, or try to, depending on how comfortable they both are. She finds him interesting, and wonders what else he is willing to tell her. They will have plenty of time to talk later. They spend the next half hour getting things she needs, mostly a few clothes and hygiene products. He makes sure she gets at least the essentials and pays for everything without hesitation.

With the bags in the Jeep, Gates says, "I know of a great diner that I think you'll like. We'll stop there on the way home, after I finish my errands."

***

Lucy's Diner is a sight for sore eyes for Trinity. She hasn't had the chance to eat in a place like it since she left North Carolina, and she immediately feels very hungry just smelling the aromas. The diner is a large establishment, the atmosphere homey and comfortable.

Once they are seated and order their drinks, Gates asks, "How long has it been since you've had southern cooking?"

"It's been too long. When I lived in Colorado, the food was pretty close at some restaurants, but just wasn't the same. There are a lot of places I missed that I couldn't find out there or in Connecticut. It's amazing how hard it was to find certain foods I love. So, with that being said, I believe I want some bacon, first and foremost, and without doubt a large plate of sausage gravy and biscuits."

Gates laughs and says, "I think you'll love it here then."

She smiles at him and admits to herself that she likes his laugh. Okay, his eyes too, but that is all she will acknowledge, at least for now. It's the first time she's heard it and she wants to hear it a lot more.

"I really like the atmosphere here. It reminds me of a small place in Asheboro. Maybe, when things smooth out a bit, we can take a drive down there."

"We may be able to. We'll have to wait and see."

Their food arrives and there isn't much talking as they eat. Trinity is getting nervous again and marks it up to exposing herself emotionally to a man she doesn't know. At the same time, she thinks Gates is probably doing the same thing. She enjoys her breakfast and while she's eating she watches him. The steak and eggs he ordered look really good, but she knows a good plate of sausage gravy and biscuits can't be beat.

She tries to observe more of the restaurant than of him. She admits the way it's setup appeals to her. Comfortable and laidback with not too much to overwhelm a customer when they walk in. Their waitress is prompt and polite. Trinity definitely wants to come back soon.

***

When they get back to the cabin, she carries her

things to her room. "I need a shower badly. I'll try not to take too long, so we can talk more if you want."

"Take your time," he replies. "We have all day."

As the hot water caresses her skin she immediately begins to feel like a new woman. She doesn't want to rush because it feels incredible, but she doesn't want to be rude either. But he did say to take her time.

By the time she turns the water off the entire bathroom is filled with steam so thick she could probably cut it with a knife. After wiping the steam off the mirror, she looks at herself and can see that her lip isn't as swollen as it was the other day. She wonders if anyone thought Gates hit her. She hopes not, but at least she doesn't have to worry about that anymore. When she stares at her brown skin and how dark it is, she thinks about how she looks standing next to him and she smiles. If things were different and they had known each other before she'd ever met Derrick, she would have gladly gone out with Gates. If things were different.

Then she thinks about her luck with men. She has a sad track record and even though he isn't a bad looking guy, she doesn't think it would work out. She also knows she doesn't want that kind of headache any longer. She shakes the thought from her head and dresses in her new clothes. When she walks back to where she thought he would be the room is empty. She hears his voice outside, figures he is on the phone and doesn't want to interrupt. Instead, she sits on the sofa, turns the television on, and waits.

"You feel better?" he asks when he walks in a few minutes later.

"You have no idea," she answers with a deep breath. "I didn't want to get out it felt so good."

"I told you to take your time. It wouldn't have been a big deal at all."

"I took long enough and didn't want to be rude. I felt like you were waiting on me."

"Not at all. Look, at least for now you are living here, so please make yourself at home and as comfortable as possible. You have no reason to be nervous around me, I promise."

"Thank you, that makes me feel better."

He sits across from her looking nervous, which surprises her.

"Okay," he begins, "I think now is as good a time as any to talk if you are comfortable with it."

She knows it needs to happen, but that doesn't stop her from being anxious. She nods in agreement. Her curiosity about him reaches a new height. Even though he told her some things earlier, she knows there's a lot more to learn about the man sitting across from her.

"I'm as ready as I'll ever be."

With pursed lips he looks at her like he is giving the idea a second thought, but then he begins. "Well, we have already told each other a little, so I don't know how much more there is to tell you and I guess a lot will automatically come out in time, but I'll do what I can."

She almost laughs and barely catches herself. "I'm sure whatever it is will be fine. Trust me, this is a little uncomfortable for me too, but it's something we need to do."

"Agreed. You already know I was with the Navy Seals and did a tour of duty, so I'll leave out some of the rough stuff and tell you some more interesting details."

"I'm interested in whatever you want to tell me."

"Like I said, I grew up in Roanoke, which isn't a huge city but not a small one either. That's part of the reason living here is so good for me, because it provides at least a little solitude. Also, when I was growing up I was sort of a wild child. In other words, I was constantly getting into trouble. Mainly in school and at home, but a few times with the law. Thankfully nothing serious or I wouldn't have been able to go into the Marines or any other branch of service. When I graduated high school, I went to boot camp only five days later and served six years, Marines and SEALs combined. I'll stop with that part for now. I've never been married and I don't have any kids, but since I've managed to calm down over the years I wouldn't mind having one or two. I like dogs, but don't have one right now because I have been on the road so much over the past few months. I plan on getting one soon, though. I may have already told you some of that, I don't know."

Trinity sits and twirls her finger around the rim of her cup, captivated by his voice and serious composure. She enjoys listening to him talk about himself, but she can tell he is only revealing basic stuff. She doesn't interrupt because she doesn't want him to stop. She wonders if he has a soft spot in him. Maybe she'll find out if she's around long enough.

"Let's see," he continues, in thought as he looks at a spot on the floor.

She tries to not look at him in any other way except as a man put in her life to help her. The last thing she needs right now is another intimate relationship, but she can't help admiring his toned arms and muscles visible through his shirt. Obviously he works out and takes care of himself. His short, dark, curly hair and rugged jawline certainly don't hurt her eyes either, and she wonders if he has any tattoos. As soon as she catches what she's doing, she mentally kicks herself. *What is wrong with you girl? Don't ever forget what happened to you and the fact you do NOT need a man. He was put in your life to help you and that is all.* Obviously, this is something she will have to continuously remind herself of.

"I'm a pretty good cook." She hears him through her own thoughts. "I like music, so occasionally you might hear me jamming out to something, and sometimes I like to watch a good movie."

She waits to see if he will say anything else, but he looks at her and apparently, that is all he will say for now.

"My turn, I guess," she says, watching his expression.

"I wouldn't mind knowing a few things about you."

She grins and says, "Well, you only told me minor things. I mean, no offense, but it seemed like you were very choosy about what you said, and I can understand. I know it will take time to get used to each other, but I will tell you a few things too.

Hopefully, they will seem interesting."

He stretches his legs and crosses his feet and arms and gives her a slight grin. She can see a glimmer in his eyes as if she sparked something in him.

She scoots back on the couch and begins. "Like I told you already, I'm from North Carolina, but lived in Colorado for a while. I moved to Connecticut with hopes of a career in photography, which began to really get going until I got mixed up with the wrong guy. I love nature and taking pictures of just about anything, but especially people and nature and animals. Ummm, I love good music, especially gospel, Motown, R&B, and I know this will shock you—I even like some country and rock and roll from time to time."

When she says that he smiles. "Yeah, to be honest I am surprised by that, I'm sorry to say."

She grins and continues. "I thought you would be. Let's see, what else? I make an awesome homemade lasagna, I love cats, and wouldn't mind a dog. Movies are addicting when I spoil myself long enough, and of course—naps. That's all I'm revealing for now."

"That's it, huh?" he asks. "Nothing about where you grew up? I mean details like what you were like growing up. You must have been an angel I guess, huh?"

Laughing at him she says, "I gave you about as much as you gave me."

"Okay, fair is fair. We can do a little at a time. Besides, I'm sure as we work together a lot will become obvious if we learn to relax around each other."

"There you go mentioning working together again. What exactly are you talking about when you say that?"

"I have some ideas that will help you in more than one way. I'm working on a plan, and I will discuss it more tonight during supper—after you fix that awesome lasagna you mentioned."

She laughs out loud again. "Oh really? Is that your way of asking me nicely to cook you dinner?"

He tries to appear shy, but doesn't do a good job with it.

"I have everything you'll need. At least I think I do, and if I don't I will go and get it if you tell me what's missing."

"I still don't think that's asking," she teases.

"Okay, okay. Will you please make me some lasagna? I'm a growing boy and I haven't had the pleasure of having a talented woman cook a good meal for me in a long time. Please."

She giggles at him and he laughs with her. Trinity feels some of the tension leave the room, and believes Gates must feel the same way.

"I guess that was good enough. I will go and take a look and see what you have and let you know if I need anything."

"Thank you kindly."

***

Gates

Later, the cabin is filled with the tang of spices,

Italian sauce, and music. The air outside is just the right temperature to have the windows open as they eat. The mild scent of pine needles wafts into the kitchen and mingles with the aroma of dinner. Even though they don't open up much more about their personal lives, they do enjoy a little conversation, mainly talking about music, movies, and foods they like.

He helps her wash the dishes then they both grab a beer and sit down to go over the plan he has written out for her. She sits next to him and even though supper still lingers in the air, he can smell her fragrance that overpowers it all. Their arms accidently touch and he feels a spark between them, but doesn't say anything. *Did she feel it too?*

He quickly discusses his plan with her before he starts to develop any emotions. He will not allow himself to feel more than he already does. When he finishes, they go to their separate rooms, leaving Gates feeling confused and irritated. *It can't happen. Neither of us is ready and it isn't a good time. Attracted or not, it can't happen.*

Chapter Five

Trinity

It's seven o'clock in the morning when Gates wakes Trinity up, and she isn't very happy about it. He firmly knocks on her door, disturbing her deep, dreaming slumber.

"Breakfast is ready. Get up and get dressed," he says from the other side of the door.

"Well, that's a little rude," she mumbles as she drags herself from beneath the covers. She walks out to the kitchen to see a bowl filled with diced fruit and a box of cereal with milk sitting on the table. She pours herself a cup of coffee and sits across from him.

"So this is breakfast?" she asks with an obvious frown.

"I thought we would keep it simple in the mornings. After we do a workout we'll have lunch, so you can have a bigger meal then. It's not good to work-out on a full stomach."

Trinity isn't awake enough to care, and she's not in the mood to even hear his voice, but keeps her opinion to herself. Instead, she pushes the cereal to the side and eats some of the fruit. She looks out the window and the day is starting out beautifully. Outside at least. The idea of working out so early in the morning wasn't very high on her to-do list. After they finish eating, she follows him outside to the back yard. He shows her some stretches, explaining they will help prevent pulled muscles and cramps. She does as he instructs, but not without groaning out loud in protest. When they are done stretching, he shows her the basement with the weight machine, a treadmill, and a stationary bike.

"You have a great setup down here," she tells him with more enthusiasm.

"Thanks. I don't use them as often as I used to, but with you here I have every intention of getting back to my old routine. I don't expect you to be able to keep up with everything that I do. Plus, for the next few days you will be sore, so don't be surprised tomorrow when you wake up."

"Good to know. Something else to look forward to," she replies with a touch of sarcasm.

He ignores her remark. "You can start easy, walking on the treadmill and work up to a decent run."

As she starts, she tries to get into a more positive attitude because she knows the mentality of exercise is important, but she finds it hard to do. Trying to think of encouraging things isn't working and she thinks about Derrick. The more she thinks about him the angrier she gets, and her anger pushes her

51

harder. She increases the speed on the belt of the treadmill; before she knows it she runs over four miles and is drenched in sweat.

"Good job on your first run," Gates tells her, obviously impressed.

Wiping her face with a towel, she mumbles, "Thanks."

"You feel like continuing?"

"Sure. I think I'll try the machines if you'll show me what to do."

"Okay, but don't over-do it."

He takes his time and explains the importance of starting out light, and how many reps and sets she needs to do. He carefully observes her expressions which imply she's angry at something or someone.

Once they're finished in the basement, what she now not-so-affectionately calls "the sweat lodge," she jumps in the shower. The high-pressure water feels wonderful as it hits her tired body. That's the first time she has worked out in years. She knows she went overboard, but at the time it felt great working out some of her hidden pain.

Gates is right about tomorrow, though. She knows she'll regret it when she rolls out of bed, but she won't stay sore. Hopefully the kinks will work themselves out within a week. He still hasn't explained why he has this plan; last night he didn't go into much detail. She wants to ask him about it today.

She dresses comfortably in shorts and a t-shirt and returns to the living room but Gates is not around. She sees a note on the table; he says he has some important business to tend to and will be back in a couple of hours. Instead of relaxing on the sofa, she takes the opportunity to walk around the cabin, study the details, and learn how he was living before she interrupted his life. From what she's seen, Gates' place is almost as beautiful as some of the pictures in magazines. She wonders where he gets the money to afford a place like this. *He said he does side work as a handyman, but does he make that much money? Maybe he also gets paid by the government from being in the Seals.*

The entire place is kept clean, almost spotless. The kitchen counters are a dark marble and all of the appliances are top grade. A chef could have a ball in there.

Trinity walks through the living room, observing the beams that travel along the ceiling and all sides of the room. Fancy is what comes to mind, especially with the oak tables and leather furniture. She strolls around the room and looks at the pictures hanging on the walls. There aren't a lot, but enough to show he isn't a hermit. When she sees one of him standing at attention in his dress blues, she's impressed.

"Very handsome," she whispers, and stands there for a moment staring at him. She wonders what the occasion was. She doesn't know a lot about the military, but she knows they only wear the dress uniforms on special occasions. *I will have to remember to ask him about it.*

She doesn't want to explore too much and feel intrusive. There isn't much else to see except his bedroom, and she has no intention of entering his personal space.

She feels a little confined, and doesn't like it. She wants to talk about any actual rules for her. She senses she isn't supposed to do anything other than what he says and that is hardly going to work. She just got away from being controlled, and she refuses to be controlled now.

Trinity wants to get out and see the outdoors and experience some culture. With all the nature surrounding her and the lake nearby, there's plenty of photographic material. She misses having a camera. She knows she will be here for a while, and thinks she should try to find a job.

She wants to be able to come and go as she pleases; having a car to drive would be nice.

She's tired and can feel the ache from the morning workout in her muscles. She turns the television on and finds an old black and white movie she hasn't seen in years, and stretches out on the sofa. Within minutes, the movie is the last thing she sees as her eyelids close and she falls into a well-earned sleep.

***

Trinity is woken by a wet tongue rapidly licking her face. She jerks awake and cries out in surprise. It certainly isn't something she expected since she thought she was alone, but when she raises her head she is staring directly into the eyes of a German shepherd puppy, tail wagging. Trinity blinks and sits up, wiping the dog's saliva from her face.

"Where did you come from, little one?" she asks the puppy and looks for Gates. She thinks he's pulling a joke on her and he's probably hiding somewhere, but there is no sign of him. She reaches down and scratches the puppy on its head, and it reacts with pure joy. A moment later she hears the kitchen door open and footsteps come her way.

"Oh, I see you two have met."

"You could say that," she giggles. "He, or she, woke me from a nap by licking me to death."

He laughs. "It's a she, and I could use a little help naming her, if you don't mind. I thought of a few names, but I don't think they fit her."

"Oh, come on it can't be that hard," Trinity replies, continuing to love on the dog. Having the puppy here brings more excitement than she would have thought. "As a little girl I used to have a dog that I loved. Her name was Sheeba. What do you think of that name?"

Sitting across from them, he wears an expression of thought and a smile at the same time. "I like it. Sheeba it is."

Trinity gets up from the sofa and Sheeba follows her as if she was her momma.

"Come on girl, let's go outside. Does she have any food?" she asks on her way through the kitchen.

"Of course not. I got her with no intention of feeding her," Gates jokes.

"Well, excuuuse me," she says and rolls her eyes.

"I actually fed her already. I want her on a schedule so she doesn't grow up to be fat."

"Of course. If you don't mind I'm taking her out to play."

***

Gates

"Go right ahead," he tells her and smiles.

He had hoped Trinity would like having a puppy around. He wanted to surprise her and his plan worked. He knew having a dog would be very therapeutic for them both. That's the biggest reason he left earlier. Even though he intended to get a dog anyway, he didn't plan on it so soon; with Trinity here it's probably a good thing.

He stands on the back porch watching them play. Trinity is running slowly as the puppy chases after her. The sound of her laughter is music to his ears. He is surprised—he didn't realize how much he missed a woman's laughter. Sitting down, he thinks about what they have talked about so far. He doesn't normally open up to a stranger, let alone anyone in particular, but he is comfortable with Trinity. He finds that a little odd, but accepts it for what it is. He watches her pick the puppy up, Sheeba licks her face, and Gates sees the biggest grin so far.

"Oh, yeah. This is definitely the right thing," he quietly says to himself.

***

Trinity

Sheeba lies on the floor chewing on a double knotted rope Gates bought. Trinity grins as she watches the puppy enjoy herself. It's a good time to talk to Gates about what is on her mind, what she was thinking earlier while he was out. She studies him as he scans through some bills, and almost chickens out because she doesn't want to be rude. She's never been good about being the one to bring things up with a man, especially one she isn't yet comfortable with. She sits back and tries to think of a good way to start off when he seems to pick up on her nervousness.

"I get the feeling you want to talk about something."

Surprised, Trinity asks, "What makes you think that?"

"Just a feeling I guess, plus you keep moving around in your chair like you have ants in your pants. What's on your mind?"

She takes a deep breath and looks at her entwined fingers.

"Okay, hold on a second," he states. "I want to tell you something."

She looks back up at him. "Okay…"

"You've only been here two days, so it's normal for us to be a little shy with opening up and being ourselves. That takes time for everyone, but I want you to know that you are living here now, at least until you are able to either get a place of your own or whatever else you choose to do. So, until then I think you should know that you have no reason to not be yourself. You have no reason to be nervous around me. I won't hurt, judge, or bite you. So, spit it out. What do you want to talk to me about?"

She stares at him, a little dumbfounded, then

collects herself. "You make it sound so easy." He sits back in his chair, puts down the papers he's holding, and focuses on her.

"It'll get easier if you let it. I know you have been hurt by men and your trust level is most likely pretty low right now. I get that, but you are sitting in a situation that will help you and hopefully you will grasp that with open arms and take advantage of it."

Nodding in agreement she responds, "You're right."

"So, talk to me," he tells her in a softer tone.

"Well, when I got out of the shower today and you were gone to do whatever you had to do, obviously one of those things was getting a dog, I had a little time to think about a couple of things that are important to me."

"Okay, I'm listening."

She tries not to be, but she can't help it—she's nervous. She tries looking into his eyes; it's hard for her but she lifts her gaze and meets his, only to feel her heart beat faster.

"What exactly is going to happen with me here?" she manages to blurt out. "I mean, I know you have a workout plan and that's all good and everything, but am I stuck here in the house all the time? Will I get to leave at all? We haven't really talked about it, but I would like to think I will be able to get out and see the trees, the hills, go to some stores. I hope to be able to get another camera and start taking pictures. That's my passion and I miss it. I have money, but can't touch it so working would be good and I know I don't have a car, but I do know how to drive."

Gates watches her as she speaks openly to him. He nods his head in acknowledgement of her feelings. He rubs his eyes before setting his elbows on the edge of the table and looking at her. "You have every right to feel that way, and of course to want and need to get out of here. I'm sorry you feel stuck. I can't say that I can relate, but I do understand. In no way are you restricted here or held captive, but let me try to make you understand something. I have been in this situation once before, helping someone. For a week or so I think it's best to lay low. Only for a week or so."

"Can I ask why?"

"Because neither of us fully know what might happen. From what you told me I get the gut feeling that your boyfriend won't give up so easily. I wouldn't be surprised if he tries to find you. For now, I think it's a good idea to wait and see if anything happens. If nothing happens by the time you are here for, let's go ahead and say two weeks, then you can go out and do some sightseeing. Even after two weeks there's still a chance he will want to find you. You just never know about guys like him. Don't get me wrong; there will be a lot of times I will go somewhere and you can go with me. We'll get out and do something fun, too, if you want."

Trinity isn't happy about staying cooped up for two weeks, even if she can go with him sometimes, but he does make sense. And, thinking about it, two weeks isn't really that long. She sulks and twiddles her fingers and waits to see if he has anything else to add. Sheeba begins nudging Trinity's leg, letting her know it's time to pay her some attention. She reaches down and rubs Sheeba's head, cooing at her.

***

Gates

Gates smiles at the two of them and struggles with his feelings. He knows it's good that things are getting out in the open between him and Trinity, and he agrees with what she brought to the table. In a way, he feels sorry for her. He would hate to be in her shoes and feel that helpless at any time in his life. He will probably feel the same way when he gets old, if he makes it that far. He needs to get her out of the house for a while; they will need to figure something out for dinner soon.

"Are you getting close to being hungry?" he asks her.

"Not really, surprisingly enough. Why, are you? We have plenty of lasagna left over."

"Actually, I was thinking it would be a good idea to get you out for a few hours. I know a good place we can go and enjoy some dinner and a few drinks if you want."

Her smile immediately brightens the room more than the overhead light, or maybe it's just his heart telling him that. *I have to control myself, no matter how beautiful she is.*

"I would love that, thank you. I'll go get ready."

He watches her walk away, and of course Sheeba follows. He snickers at this. Sheeba connects with her, not him. She's obviously going to be more her dog than his.

***

Trinity

At the Lakeside Bar and Grill, Gates orders a beer and Trinity asks for a Long Island Iced Tea.

"I'm not much of a drinker. I don't like the way I feel when I'm drunk, but the main reason is I struggle to reconcile drinking alcohol with my faith," she says.

"So, you see yourself as a Christian?" Gates asks.

"Well, I haven't been to church in a while because Derrick didn't like me going. Every time I wanted to go he would get angry about it. The last time I asked him if I could go, he hit me and knocked me to the floor."

He scoffs and shakes his head in disbelief. "That's a shame, in my opinion. I don't think it's right for anyone to control someone. Especially if they say they care about you, and to hit you for it pisses me off, to be honest. In my opinion a man who beats on a woman is nothing more than a bully, and most bullies are cowards."

She can hear his tone rise when he speaks, and for some odd reason it comforts her. "I agree, thank you."

"Do you want to get back into church?"

She nods. "When I was at Howard and Mattie's house I felt a little weird about it all. But then I thought, why would I feel weird about any of it? I guess it was because God was pulling on me and I felt guilt about not going, I don't know, but yeah, I want too. My momma raised me to believe in God, but when I moved out on my own, life got busy and I left church and God behind. Probably a big reason why so much went wrong."

"Don't be so hard on yourself. Life happens. All you can do now is move forward and if you feel you need to get back in church and live the way you believe, then do it."

She lowers her eyes and thinks. She knows he's right, and she can feel God tugging on her heart. She knows she isn't a bad person, but she also knows being good isn't enough. There's a lot more to being a Christian than that.

"I have some thinking to do I guess," she responds. "I have so much on my plate right now and I'm feeling overwhelmed."

The waitress brings their drinks and says she'll be back in a few minutes to take their dinner order. They sip at their drinks without saying anything. She feels good inside knowing she has his support. He surprises her with his next words.

"If you want to go to church Sunday, I'll let you use the car so you can go."

"Are you sure?"

"I only ask that you promise me you won't go anywhere else without me, like we talked about earlier. I only say that because I don't want anything to happen to you."

"I promise, if I go. I don't know yet."

She can't believe it. He is actually trusting her

with one of his cars. Her heart beats faster than before and she suddenly feels guilty about drinking. She pushes it from her, wishing she hadn't ordered it.

"You okay?" he asks.

"Yeah, I'm good. I just don't want it after all. I think I'll get a Sprite or something else instead."

Trinity has no intention of letting guilt or her decision not to drink ruin her evening. She will enjoy a great meal with great company. When their waitress returns, she asks for a steak, cooked medium-well, with a baked potato. Gates orders a steak, well-done. As they eat, they watch a few couples enjoying the small dance floor. She thinks about how nice it would be if Gates asked her to dance, but doesn't think he will. She thinks maybe one day something with someone will happen, but it won't be any time soon.

Chapter Six

Derrick

Derrick sits in his apartment alone as the darkness envelopes him. The feelings that flow through him are eating him from the inside out, and the only way he can deal with them is by drinking. It isn't the best way, but he's at a loss and the wracking pain is too much to bear otherwise. He thinks about selling the drugs he stashed away, but he knows the risks and consequences, and the idea of becoming his own best customer isn't appealing.

He considers hiring a private detective to find Trinity. He needs to either have her with him or let her know she's making a huge mistake by leaving him; she won't like the way he'll tell her that. In his hand is the phone number for someone named David Tremper, a recommendation from a friend. He's local, and the biography on his website makes him look good. Derrick will call him tomorrow. Calling him when he's drunk isn't a good idea; he wants to be clear-headed when he talks to this David Tremper.

Derrick stumbles into the spare room with the pool table. He hopes shooting some balls for a while will get his mind off her. Turning the stereo up loud, swallowing a mouthful of his beer, and taking a cue off of the wall, he stands and stares blindly at the scattered balls. He remembers how she felt when he bought it. She didn't want him to get the table because it's another way he can have his friends over, but he didn't care. He works hard for his money and he pays all the bills, so he is going to do what he wants whether she likes it or not.

He tried hard to make her happy, or at least he thought so, but apparently she wasn't. He gave her everything she wanted, even if she did make good money with her photography hobby. She hates it when he calls it a hobby. He knows she has some money saved somewhere, but if she's smart she won't take it out. Any kind of transactions will leave a trail and he doesn't think she is that stupid. Anyhow, if he hires the detective, she will eventually be found, no matter where she is hiding.

After racking the balls he finishes the rest of his beer, chalks his cue, and bends over the edge of the table. He closes one eye to get a decent focus; he's had so much to drink the balls are blurry. He breaks with enough force it sounds as if a gun went off, making him smile. Derrick walks around the table observing each possible shot, but something feels off. Something is missing. Music. He needs different music. Something with a better beat to it.

For the next few hours he listens to reggae and

rap, bobbing his head, getting drunker and playing pool. The more he drinks the more shots he misses, but he doesn't care. By the time he crashes on the soft leather couch he doesn't care about much of anything. Except finding Trinity.

***

Trinity

Trinity thinks about the past few hours—how comfortable she felt when out with Gates. She's beginning to think it will all be okay, but she refuses to get her hopes up too much. She learned the hard way to not do that.

Lying in bed, she listens to the rain that started shortly after they got home. Sheeba is lying on the floor beside the bed. She tried to jump up on the bed with Trinity, but she doesn't want Sheeba to get used to that. Sheeba isn't supposed to be her dog anyhow, but for some reason she instantly became attached to Trinity. She can hear Sheeba whimpering softly, hoping to get her way and Trinity smiles.

"Listen to you down there, you little beggar. Shhh, be quiet. I have to sleep, too."

Trinity tosses and turns for an hour because she can't stop thinking. So many things are going through her mind. Is Gates still awake? What is he thinking? What is Derrick thinking? Is he planning to find her? She has plenty of money in her bank account, but is unable to get to it. That bugs her, too. She thinks about making a withdrawal when she goes to church, but will that be a way for Derrick to find her? She should probably ask Gates. She doesn't have a good feeling about it, and she's scared to do anything without thinking it through first. She feels bad she told him she doesn't have money, but in a way she doesn't since she can't get to it.

Finally, her brain tires and her eyes stay closed. The steady sound of the rain helps Trinity relax, and Sheeba has long since stopped whining and fallen asleep. Maybe her dreams will be good to her. Maybe she'll wake up to a sunny day, both literally and figuratively.

***

Gates

Gates isn't having an easy time going to sleep, and wonders if Trinity is similarly afflicted. He looks at his alarm clock and sees it is 1:17 in the morning. The sight of that doesn't put a smile on his face. He has too many things on his mind; that's his main problem. He has to mentally sort out stuff he isn't comfortable talking about with Trinity. His attraction to her is on his mind and affecting his thought process. He is struggling with her being here. If he had known she was so attractive, he wouldn't have put himself in this situation. But he did tell Howard he would help. He just had no idea Trinity was so beautiful and would make his senses go crazy.

She is certainly a lady; he clearly sees that. He

will not in any way treat her otherwise. He thinks about their dinner conversation concerning her Christian faith. He admires that she opened up to him and held on to her beliefs. A lot of people are cautious when discussing religion, but she was honest. He also respects her for telling him she felt stuck in the house, which reminds him he offered her the use of the car. He surprised himself with that one. He hopes he didn't make the wrong decision, but will trust she has good judgement.

He can't help thinking about a friend he hasn't talked to in years, an old Seal buddy Gates served with. The things they went through together were horrendous. Gates tries not to think about those experiences—too many painful, bad memories. He doesn't know why Tommy came to mind, but maybe he should try to get in touch with him. He will have to check his contacts to see if Tommy's info is still there. He never did understand why they lost touch.

He rolls onto his stomach and tries to fall asleep. It doesn't take long, but tonight the nightmares pay him a visit. It has been a long time since he's been through that kind of pain.

The explosions wouldn't stop and the ringing in his ears was getting louder, but even with all of that he couldn't get the screaming to go away. The sound of one of the men on his team shouting for help was constant, but he couldn't find him. Where was he?

Looking around the edge of a deserted building, all he could see was more destruction and horror.

House of Refuge

The dark skies were lit up from fires that engulfed most of the buildings in the small town. Cars were lying on their side or left in the middle of the road, some of them on fire. As he searched for any sign of a sniper, he saw a child run across the street with something in his arms. What was the kid carrying? He didn't know, but in this world it could be a bomb. The kid disappeared, and Gates took the chance to run along the side of what was left of the concrete wall he had been hiding behind. Running across the alley he took another chance of being shot at, but he had to find his friend, his fellow Seal.

He could hear him screaming again, and every time Gates thought he was getting closer, he stopped and was still alone. He didn't understand why he was alone. The other four Seals on the team had disappeared. Were they dead? Were they lost? He didn't know, but he knew he had to find his buddy and get out of there, and fast. He kept a sharp eye out and kept low as he continued to run, searching behind every crevice, every wall, every obstacle. What he found wouldn't normally scare him after the horrors he had already seen. He tripped and fell face first into a bloody mess. Scrambling to gain his footing he stood, his eyes bulging as he stared at all four of his comrades. Piled one on top of the other. Blood ran freely onto the ground as he stared at them; their empty eyes pierced his soul. Before he could do anything, before he could see if even one of them was alive, a grenade landed at his feet and his entire world was filled with pain.

***

Trinity

Saturday morning it's still raining, putting a damper on doing anything outside the cabin. Trinity can't believe how much it has rained. She can't recall seeing this much of it in a long time. Gates takes Sheeba out long enough to do her business, but that's it.

After a small breakfast of fruit and toast, they go downstairs for the morning routine. Trinity isn't as sore as she thought she would be, but she still hurts enough to wince when she starts working on the weight machines. Thankfully, the tenderness works itself out and she doesn't hurt the entire time. She notices Gates is quiet and reserved. She wonders if he is upset about something and wants to ask, but waits to see if his mood changes.

Gates rides the stationary bike for five miles and then does a heavy routine on the machines as Sheeba paces around, watching both of them and getting in their way. She only wants to play, but finally gets the idea they aren't going to give her their full attention so she lies down in a corner.

Trinity observes Gates as he works out, but doesn't question him about anything. The intensity on his face almost frightens her, so she stops watching him and focuses on herself. When they are both finished, he says he is hitting the shower and goes upstairs without another word.

Through the rest of the afternoon, the rain is relentless; the news report says it should let up by late evening. Trinity hopes so; the mood in the house is dreary enough, especially with Gates' odd behavior. There isn't much else to do except watch movies. During a break between shows they call Mattie and Howard to let them know everything is going well. She tells them about her workout and how sore she is, and that she intends to go to church Sunday. They are especially happy to hear that. Then Gates takes time to talk with them.

Sheeba clings to Trinity on the sofa and Gates tries to act betrayed. Sheeba stays on the sofa, rolling her brown eyes at him as if it is obvious where she should be. Trinity laughs at them both.

His mood seems to have lightened a bit after talking to Howard and Mattie.

"I hope you don't mind, but you seemed somewhat distant this morning. Is something bothering you?"

She watches his gaze move from the television and fall to the floor. Gates doesn't say anything for a moment; she thinks maybe he won't. Then he turns and looks at her. "I'm sorry. I didn't mean to come across in a bad way. I just…" he pauses, then says, "It's been a while, but for some reason I had a nightmare last night. I didn't sleep well."

Trinity isn't sure how to respond. She thought he was upset with her. "I'm sorry. Do you want to talk about it?"

"No offense, but I'd rather not." Gates turns back to the movie.

Trinity doesn't want to push the subject or her luck, so she also turns back to watching the movie. She reminds herself they are both learning about each other, and if he ever talks to her about his nightmares it could be a long time coming. She tries to pay attention to the movie, but from time to time glances his way to see whether he is watching the movie or looking at her. She senses he is eyeing her, but doesn't catch him in the act. She doesn't want to admit her growing attraction for Gates because of her bad luck with men.

There isn't much conversation, even after the movies. It seems the weatherman was wrong because it's raining harder now than a few hours ago. Neither one of them offers to cook, so they finish up the leftover lasagna, eating quietly. When they are finished, Gates speaks.

"I'll take care of the dishes, then I'm going to bed. Again, I'm sorry. Hopefully, I'll sleep better tonight and will be in a better mood tomorrow."

"It's okay. I understand. I'm tired, so I think I'm going to go to bed too. I'll see you tomorrow. Goodnight."

"Goodnight, Trinity."

Chapter Seven

Sunday morning arrives with a brightness that fills the day, the sun gracing them with its presence. Thankfully, sometime during the night the rain finally stopped. They don't have a workout scheduled today and Trinity is grateful. She gets out of bed at 6:30, filled with anticipation. She takes Sheeba outside and has some coffee before getting ready for church. Gates wakes up while she's getting ready; she walks into the kitchen greeting him with a smile.

"Good morning," she says when she sees him staring at her, only half awake. "I hope you had a better night's sleep."

"Good morning, uhhh, yeah, much better thank you. I see you're ready to go."

"Yeah, I'm nervous though, but excited at the same time."

"Why are you nervous?" he asks, leaning against the counter, sipping his coffee.

"I don't know. I guess it's like going to a new

73

school. I will go in there not knowing anyone, so in a way I'll feel like an outsider."

"I'm sure you'll fit right in with no problems. It's church; I would like to think you'll feel welcomed."

"I'm sure I will. I'm probably overthinking it like I do a lot of things. I don't know where to go, exactly, so I guess I'll go to the one we passed the other day. I think I read on the sign that it's a Baptist church. I'll try that one."

"You remember how to get to it?"

Nodding, she replies, "Yeah, I think so."

She senses he is still looking at her; when she glances up at him he averts his eyes, like he is caught with his hands in the cookie jar. She smiles because she knows he is checking her out, and it makes her feel good. She finishes her coffee, goes to brush her teeth, then returns and asks him for the keys to the car.

"Are you certain this is okay?"

"Yeah, I'm not worried, just come home right after, if you don't mind. If you want to go somewhere else later we can go together, just to be on the safe side."

She thinks about asking him about going to the ATM, but drops it until later.

"I promise. I'll see you later, and thank you very much."

"You're welcome. Have a good time."

***

Gates

He watches her pull out of the driveway, and Sheeba whines like she already misses her. He looks down at who is supposed to be his dog, and rubs her head as he shakes his.

"She will only be gone for a little while, girl. She'll be back. You are supposed to be my dog anyhow, traitor."

She looks up at him and wags her tail, letting her tongue fall from the side of her open mouth. Gates laughs at her and asks if she wants to go out. When she hears that word she runs to the door and waits for him. He puts a leash on her because it's muddy and he doesn't want it all over her.

While they are outside, he looks at his surroundings. He sees the same things he has always seen, but in some way they feel different. The same oak, cedar, and dogwood trees are in the back yard, still glistening slightly from the morning dew. The way the sun sparkles off the ripples of the lake seems to be more profound. He suddenly realizes it isn't his surroundings; it's his life that feels different. He can't explain it. It's baffling, but he has a feeling it may have something to do with the lovely lady who just drove off in his car. He looks at Sheeba, smiles, and welcomes the change.

***

Trinity

Trinity pulls into the parking lot of the large

white church building and turns the motor off. It's been too long since she's been able to go to church, and she can feel the excitement coursing through her veins. Closing her eyes, she says a silent prayer thanking Jesus for blessing her with the opportunity to be there. He always knows what's best for her.

When she walks into the building, two ushers welcome her with smiles and hand her a pamphlet that describes the morning service. A couple of ladies walk up, introduce themselves, and make her feel at home. They tell her there is coffee in the kitchenette in the corner. She thanks them, and admires the large room where she will be able to hear a sermon for the first time in what feels like ages. Her eyes tear up from the sheer joy of being there and feeling welcome.

She forgets about the coffee and chooses to sit halfway down the aisle in one of the empty pews. Many have already arrived, standing around chatting as the choir assembles on the large stage behind the pulpit. Her heart pounds; she feels like she's getting ready to hear a concert. Moments later an older gentleman, she thinks he may be the pastor, stands behind the pulpit, sorting through his Bible and papers.

Everyone begins to find a seat. The choir stands and waits while a young woman takes her place behind the large, shiny piano and another lady sits behind an organ. She sees a few more people gather behind drums, a guitar and two microphones. Glorious music fills her ears as they play a song Trinity doesn't know, but it doesn't matter. She's in the perfect place and her soul is being filled. She couldn't be happier.

The congregation sings along with the next songs, ones she has always loved. "Amazing Grace." "Take Me as I Am." "How Great Thou Art." Tears flow as her heart beams with her love for Jesus. When the music stops, the pastor introduces himself and welcomes everyone in the room.

He lowers his head and prays; Trinity again gives thanks to God for His blessings.

Once everyone is seated the pastor begins a sermon about what it means to be a Christian in today's society and how to live daily as a Christian. Part of her feels like he is preaching directly to her, although she knows that can't be so.

He speaks about the way society is today. The temptations of the flesh, of money, pride, and envy. He touches on how hard it is to fight those temptations, but when Christians are able to turn away from them and live for Jesus Christ, it pleases Him and rewards are bountiful. He talks more about how Christians will be persecuted, ridiculed and killed in our world, but God is always with us and the gates of Heaven are waiting for us to walk through them.

When the sermon is over, the choir sings two more songs and the pastor welcomes anyone who needs prayer to walk up front and he will pray with them. With nervous hesitation, she steps out from the pew and walks to the front. She rededicates her life to Jesus and immediately feels more alive than she has in years. She cries joyful tears and even hugs the pastor afterward, surprising him. After the closing prayer, someone taps her shoulder. Trinity turns to see a woman who could easily be her mother.

"Hey, my name is Gloria Hepstrom. I wanted to welcome you and tell you I'm so glad you are here."

Grinning with a joyful heart, she replies, "Thank you, I'm glad I'm here too. I'm Trinity. This is a beautiful church. I can't believe I was able to find it."

"Are you new to the area?"

"Yes, Ma'am. I just got here a few days ago."

"I hope you like it here. Moneta is small but it's a beautiful place. Have you seen the lake yet?"

"Actually, only a little of it. I'm staying with a friend who lives right on the edge of it. I don't remember the name of the area, but yeah, it's nice. I think I'll like it here."

"Well, I know how hard it can be to make friends when you are new. Here's my number if you would like to talk or maybe meet for lunch sometime."

Trinity takes Gloria's number and thanks her. They hug and agree to talk soon, and if not they will definitely see each other next week. On her drive back to the cabin, Trinity feels completely whole. Going to church and specifically that church is obviously what she's supposed to have done this morning. So much gratitude fills her heart and she can't wait to tell Gates all about it. Hopefully, he will be open to hearing her.

***

Gates

"So you enjoyed yourself then?" Gates asks, even though it's written all over her face. He loves seeing her so excited.

"It was perfect, thank you so much for letting me take the car so I could go."

"Good, I'm glad, and you are welcome."

"I hope you don't mind me telling you the best part, the big choice I made while I was there."

"Why would I mind? What did you do?" he asks, his curiosity piqued.

Filled with energy, she paces the floor as she begins talking. "I don't know, but I was so caught up in the sermon and the music that the entire time I was there, I kept feeling God pull on my heart. At the end the pastor asked if anyone needed prayer, and if they did to walk up front. I was so nervous, but I went right up there and rededicated my life to Jesus. I feel so much better now. You have no idea."

Sitting back and watching the excitement flow from her, Gates can't help but be thrilled for Trinity. He grins, and Sheeba's obviously happy too, because she keeps jumping around wanting attention.

While Trinity scratches Sheeba behind her ears and talks to her, Gates says, "I have to admit that I don't know, but I'm glad you do."

"Do you think I will be able to use the car to go next week?"

"Of course, I don't have a problem with that at all."

"Thank you. Oh and also, a sweet woman gave me her number and said I can call since I'm new to the area. Maybe I met a new friend too. You don't mind if I use the phone sometimes, right?"

He thinks for a moment before answering. "I'm not comfortable with the house number being given out to anyone. At least not right now, but I have an even better idea. Why don't we go to town and get you a few more things? I know you need more clothes and I'll get you a prepaid phone. That way it won't be a problem."

"I would like to have a few more clothes, especially since I'm going to be going to church now. Thank you in advance for the phone, but don't you think you may be a little too cautious?"

Gates shakes his head. "I don't. Don't take it wrong, but I am accustomed to having to be this way. It's nothing against you."

"Okay."

Trinity unexpectedly gets up, walks over, and wraps her arms around him, hugging him tightly. He is caught off guard, but gladly hugs her back, wondering where this special attention comes from. The most difficult part for him is letting go. Her hair smells like flowers, and the feeling of her against him is incredible.

He smiles back at her when she pulls away. "What, may I ask, do I deserve that for?"

Grinning and looking into his eyes, she replies, "For everything you have already done and are doing. Thank you. I only want to express it by more than saying it. Plus, I'm feeling really good right now."

He can really see the gleam in her green eyes and her smile is intoxicating. He stares at her and can't help but appreciate her beauty. He's tempted to pull her into his arms again, but thinks it probably isn't a good idea.

"You're welcome," is all he can manage to say. "Ummm, if you want to take what appears to be your dog outside first, we'll go and get that phone and stuff and maybe get a bite to eat afterward."

Laughing, she heads outside and Sheeba follows her to the back yard. He watches her with the dog and wonders what is happening. She has found God again and is obviously excited about it. She is in his life, and if he's honest with himself, he is beginning to feel very good about her being there, no matter what the future holds for either of them. He remembers how he felt earlier while he was outside with Sheeba. The idea that God placed them together came to mind as well as curiosity. He wonders about the whole church thing. He can feel his attraction for her growing as he watches, and once again he has to remind himself that something intimate isn't something she needs, nor does he. Or does he?

***

Trinity

Trinity stands on the back deck and watches Sheeba sniff around the yard, searching for the perfect place to do what needs to be done. Her back is to the house, but if Gates could see her, he would see a smile covering her entire face. It was unexpected, but giving him a hug felt perfect and completely right. She only hopes it was right for him as well. She thinks so by the look that was on his face. *Then again, it's probably just the fact that I'm feeling so great at the moment.* She giggles and tells Sheeba to hurry and find a place to go. The dog looks at her as if she is telling her to be patient.

Trinity thinks about how fast things are happening and wonders if she should be more cautious. She is letting her emotions get away from her; she can tell that even though she and Gates don't know each other very well, something is happening between them. *Then again, it's been so long since anything good has been in my life, maybe I don't really know how or what I feel.* Confused, she again tells Sheeba to hurry. A couple of minutes later they walk back inside to find Gates ready to go.

Her stomach begins to growl as they drive away, confirmation that lunch will be first, then shopping.

***

Derrick

Almost eight hundred miles north, a private detective is talking to Derrick. "So, we are perfectly clear, I will not in any fashion approach her, either in person or phone or any other way. My only job is to find her and tell you where she is. Is that clear between us?" the detective asks.

Derrick breathes into the phone and answers,

"Yes, crystal clear. I'm sending the money now. You should have it in a few minutes. Call me as soon as you find something on her."

He ends the call without waiting for a response, punches in the required amount of five thousand dollars into the computer, and hits enter. Half now and the other half when Trinity is found. Paying a private detective to find her will put a large dent in his savings, but she will be found. It may take a little time, but he will get her back.

***

Trinity

That night she gives in and lets Sheeba sleep on the bed with her. Trinity is immediately delighted. She quickly discovers how much of a cuddler and source of comfort a dog can be. The only hard part is getting the puppy to calm down and stop giving her kisses. Once she manages to get Sheeba to lie still, Trinity stares up at the ceiling. The only light is outside, but it isn't coming directly through the window. It's cool enough to have the window open; there is a gentle breeze and she hears the crickets playing their song. She always loved listening to them as a little girl. She really misses home.

She remembers when she was little how badly she wanted to hurry up and get old enough to leave Asheboro, but now she knows how silly that was. She was only five years old. She misses everything about being there, at least what she can remember of it. She wonders sometimes how her friends are and if they still live there. Probably not many, since it was so long ago.

She'll get depressed if she thinks too much about what she has let go of in her life, but now she feels like she might have a new start. A new beginning. Now that she's in Virginia she isn't too far away from where she used to live in North Carolina. So many things have changed since the last time she was there. She isn't close to anyone in her family, and since her momma passed,

Trinity only wants to reconnect. If that's even possible.

She reflects on what happened earlier in the day and her heart beams. This was the best day she's had in a long time. Being able to go to church and feeling so welcome, re-dedicating her life to Jesus Christ, making a new friend, and telling Gates all about it.

Then the shopping. He was going to take her to Walmart in Bedford, but changed his mind and went all the way to Roanoke. He must have been in a great mood because he let her pick out five outfits, two pairs of dress shoes, two dresses, a purse, make-up and a pre-paid phone. She felt like it was Christmas. She feels guilty about how much Gates is spending on her, but she did talk about her bank account with him and told him she would pay him back when it's safe. He didn't seem concerned about the money at all.

"You can help me out around the house a little and cook some more great meals if you really want to pay me back."

"So another words you want a maid and a chef."

He laughed and replied, "Well, that would be fantastic, but I won't put a label on it. Just mentioning it is all."

Laughing, Trinity said, "You take my jokes too seriously. I'm more than happy to help out. It's the least I can do for everything you're doing for me."

"Tomorrow, we'll get back into our scheduled routine. I also want to start teaching you some beginner's Tai Chi. It's great for stress and helps with muscle tone. We both need it."

Before she falls asleep she remembers one other detail about the day. She thinks about the way she felt in his arms when she hugged him, and the way he looked back at her. She likes that feeling. A lot.

Chapter Eight

This morning, before she does anything else, Trinity gets on her knees and talks to God. She has decided to start every day talking to Him; she wants to make prayer her first priority. There is no better way to start her day. Afterward, she dresses and takes Sheeba out, shivering with the slight chill in the air. She won't stay that way, though, once she starts her workout with Gates. When she goes back inside he is making coffee. "Hey, how did you sleep last night?" he asks.

"I slept like a rock, especially with little miss priss here. She's a fantastic source of heat. How about you?"

Laughing, he replies, "I slept good. I'm ready for the day. Well, I should say once I get some coffee in me I will be. Are you still sore from the other day?"

"Ehhh, it's not as bad as it was, so I guess I'm ready for another day of it."

"Good."

They enjoy their coffee on the deck, watching the birds in the trees and talking about nothing in particular. Sheeba surprises them with her speed when a squirrel makes the mistake of running across the yard. They yell at her to leave the poor squirrel alone, but it's like yelling at a brick wall—a waste of time. Thankfully, the small animal runs up a tree and away from danger.

Once Sheeba tires herself out from excitement, they coax her into the house and down to the basement. Gates shows Trinity some Tai Chi basics—how to stand with her feet firmly planted and how to feel centered. She follows his every move as he shows her how to move her arms and hands, how to bend at the knees and swivel, and most importantly how to breathe in steady rhythms. They work on Tai Chi for half an hour; even though it's slow, Trinity can feel the benefits. Next up is cardio, and she tires quickly.

"Do we have to do any more today?" she asks him, hoping he will say no.

"You giving up on me already?" he asks, wiping the sweat off his forehead with an old towel that hung from a bench.

"I'm sorry, but I'm really tired for some reason."

"It's okay, it takes time to get used to. We can stop for the day if you want."

"Thank you. I guess I'll use the lame excuse of it being a Monday."

"Yeah, that's a good one," he snickers.

***

Gates

Later that day Gates thinks again about how he acted toward Trinity when he was tired and had a nightmare. He isn't used to explaining himself, but he feels not only should he talk to her about it, but it will be good to get it off his mind. He walks to her room and knocks on her door.

"Come in."

Pushing the door open, he sees she is reading and hesitates. "Hey, I'm sorry to disturb you, but I was wondering if I can talk to you about something."

"Sure, come on in," she tells him and slides her feet off the bed. "Have a seat. What's up?"

Sitting on the edge he folds his hands and looks at the floor. Not sure exactly how to start, he begins with an apology.

"I've been thinking about Saturday, how I acted because of my nightmare and not sleeping well. I want to say I'm sorry."

"I appreciate that, but you really don't have to. I mean, I can't relate to what you went through overseas, but I can imagine how horrible it had to be."

Nodding, he agrees things were rough. "Still, I want to."

***

Trinity

She feels he wants to say more and asks, "Do you want to talk about the nightmare? I'm all ears if

88

you need to."

"This isn't something I have an easy time talking about, but I feel like I can with you."

She watches his expressions. With pursed lips she leans forward, takes his hand in hers and waits patiently. Her heart goes out to him, sensing his struggle.

"Sometimes I have nightmares that put me in the middle of a war zone." In vivid detail, he tells her about an experience with the rest of his team, four other Seals. "We were walking through buildings that had already been destroyed and blown up. We saw bodies lying around, most of them in pieces. In some of my dreams, I see one of the guys I went through boot camp with walking toward me with only one arm, holding the other in his spare hand. He is covered in blood and talks about going home, then walks away. Then a child looks up at me from beneath a sheet of stone, obviously crushed by an explosion, and cries out to me, begging for help in his native language. That's usually when I wake up, and can't go back to sleep."

By the time he finishes, his hands are shaking. Trinity wipes the tears from her eyes. She scoots closer to Gates and wraps her arms around him, squeezing him tightly.

"I'm so sorry you are struggling. Thank you for talking to me about it. It takes courage to talk about your demons."

He hugs her back. "Thank you for being here."

"Anytime you want to talk please let me know."

Standing, he looks at her and smiles. "I will, and the same goes for you. I'm going to go for a walk, I think."

The weeks go by and even after a month there aren't any major differences in their schedules. In the mornings, they eat a small breakfast of fruit or cereal, then work out. Sometimes one or both will take a nap afterward. Some days they go out for a bite to eat or drive around to enjoy the country air and scenery. Sometimes she cooks dinner, but he also enjoys cooking once in a while. One evening he makes a delicious beef stew from scratch. She makes sure to tell him it was the best stew she has ever had.

The one thing Trinity always does is pray—she talks to God in the mornings when she wakes up, at night when she goes to bed, and throughout the day. She decides she needs a Bible. She hasn't seen one in the house, so she doesn't know if Gates even owns one. Tomorrow is Sunday and she's excited. She'll be able to go to church and hear the choir, hear the gospel of Jesus Christ, and praise Him. Plus, she will see Gloria again. They have talked a few times and are becoming friends, something Trinity definitely needs.

She has been living with Gates for a little over a month, and the tension between them seems to have totally disappeared. They have grown accustomed to being around each other, knowing when to give space and when to talk and laugh. Because they have so quickly become comfortable with each other, Trinity notices her growing attraction to Gates, and thinks he's starting to feel the same way. She thinks about the nights they watch movies together and the way he looks at her when she catches him staring. He's so cute when he looks away, getting shy with her.

She has to admit she likes the way he looks. Even if she didn't know him and just saw him on the street, she would know he took great care of himself. She wonders if there is a chance for them to have something together, but maybe she really shouldn't think that way. She just got out of something horrible and doesn't know him well enough. But she also wonders if God put her with Gates in particular for that very reason. She will pray about it, knowing even after getting an answer from God temptations will still be there. *Especially when he walks out of the bathroom without his shirt on. Is he trying to tease me?*

It's already evening and she should start getting ready for bed soon. Sheeba is lying by her feet, tired from the day. Trinity can't stop thinking about Gates; she wants to walk in and talk to him about how she feels. What should she do? She starts biting her nails then realizes what she's doing and shakes her head. It won't be easy to just walk in and bring it up, but she feels like she should get it off her shoulders.

***

Gates

Reading before bed isn't why he wants to be alone in his room. It isn't even something he does normally. He told Trinity he wants to read, but he knows he's basically hiding. The real reason is being around her is difficult because of his increasing attraction. Earlier, when she came out of her room after her shower she smelled so good he wanted to pull her in his arms and hold her. He wanted to be hypnotized by her fragrance, the feel of her body against his, and to be completely honest—he desperately wanted to kiss her. That's why he is alone in his room. That's why he is acting like a teenager.

He knows he should talk to her about it and wonders how she feels toward him. *What will she say if I tell her I'm attracted to her?* No, he should rephrase that. *What will she think if I tell her I think she's the most beautiful woman I have ever seen, and my feelings for her are growing?*

She's hard to read so he isn't sure if he should say anything or not. Yes, she has become comfortable with him and has opened up a lot. Yes, they are doing things together and he thinks he has seen her looking at him in ways that can send certain messages. But he knows himself; he's probably reading more into those looks than he should. He has to do something before he loses his mind. The last thing he will ever do is disrespect her in any way.

"Are you enjoying your book?"

He's caught off guard when he hears her sweet, soft voice from the doorway. He was deep in thoughts about her when she appeared, and she giggles when he jumps.

"Oh, hey I didn't hear you," he says with a grin and sits up on the edge of the bed.

"Sorry about that."

He lays the book he isn't actually reading on the bed and looks at her smiling at him. "No, I wasn't really getting into it, so it's okay. What are you doing?"

"I was lonely in there and thought if you weren't too involved with your book, maybe we could talk. If that's okay."

"Of course, come on in," he replies and pats the edge of the bed.

He watches her walk toward him and feels his heart hammer against his chest. He wouldn't be surprised if she can hear it. To him it sounds like the drums in Jumanji. She's wearing light green pajamas with little red hearts all over them, and with the way her hips sway she looks like a Victoria's Secret model.

***

Trinity

She sees how he looks at her and doesn't try to hide her smile. Her nerves are going crazy, and when she gets next to the bed she thinks she feels the temperature rise in the room. She sits about two feet away, because she's afraid if she sits too close, something will happen that neither will be able, or want, to stop.

"What's on your mind?" he asks.

She looks at the floor and wonders how she's going to start. She takes a deep breath and silently asks God to guide her. Her fingers play with the cuffs of her sleeves; she's obviously nervous.

93

"It's nothing really…well, it is, but I guess I only want to talk is all. I guess being in there alone isn't enough for me tonight."

He smiles and asks, "What do you mean?"

She looks into his eyes and her heart clenches. "Well, ummm…"

"Do you want to watch a movie or something?"

Something? Yeah I guess you could say that. "No, not really in the mood for a movie."

"Are you sure you are okay? Correct me if I'm wrong, but you are acting like you really have something on your mind. You can talk to me. You never know, I might be able to relate."

Is that a hint?

He surprises her by placing his hand on her back. She can feel the warmth of it through her shirt, sending a jolt through her. She's surprised she didn't jump. She stares into his eyes and knows she has to be honest with him. Right then.

"Okay, please don't take this the wrong way, Gates, but there is something that's very much on my mind and I don't know any way to tell you but to be honest about it."

"Okay, I'm all ears."

"Trust me when I say this, because of what I have been through with men that I am very surprised, but I've become very attracted to you and I don't know what to do about it. I'm a Christian and I don't want to do anything to feel bad about. Does that make sense?"

***

Gates

He almost blows out the air he was holding in, but manages to start breathing again without letting her notice. He was scared she was going to say something he wasn't prepared to hear. Even though he was hoping she felt the same as him, he is still surprised she wants to talk about it.

"It makes perfect sense, and I can't express how relieved I am to hear you say that."

"Why?"

"Because I've been struggling with the same feelings about you, but I didn't want to touch you or hold you or anything else because I didn't know how you felt. I didn't want to scare you. I didn't know what was in your mind or heart. All I knew for sure was the pain you have been through, but I had hope."

"I'm scared, Gates."

"Of me?" he asks, with a look of hurt on his face.

"Oh, no, no, definitely not! I'm sorry," she exclaims and holds his hand in hers. "I'm scared because I don't know what to do. I don't know if God planned this, if I'm supposed to be here right now talking to you about this, if something is supposed to happen between us, or what. I'm just not sure about anything right now except that I would really like it…if you held me."

When Trinity says those words and he sees the expression on her face his desire to hold her turns into a need. She doesn't have to make that request again. He moves closer and wraps his arms around her slim waist, pulling her to him. Her hands rest against his chest and her head is on his shoulder. Neither say a word; they simply enjoy each other's presence and the feel of being in each other's arms. Even though he knows they are both confused about the entire situation, holding her is definitely right. Perfect. He can feel her hot breath through his shirt and her hands pressed between them. He takes a chance and kisses her on her forehead.

She lifts her head and looks into his eyes and he sees it. There's passion in her eyes. Very obvious passion. Obvious and dangerous. She lowers her hungry eyes to his lips and he takes that as an invitation to taste hers. Their lips meet for the first time; they know it will not be the last, but they can't stay that way. He enjoys the passion they share, but too soon, she breaks away.

Shaking her hands and stepping away from the bed, Trinity apologizes vehemently. "Oh, my goodness! I'm so sorry, I'm so sorry!"

"Don't be sorry, please," he pleads as he stands with her. He wants to hold her again, but knows she needs her space.

Turning toward him she cries, "I'm not sorry for what happened; I'm sorry for having to pull away." Tears run down her flushed cheeks and her chest heaves. "Please don't be mad."

"Hey…" he says softly and steps closer, standing only inches away. With a single finger beneath her quivering chin, he lifts her face to look into her eyes. "I'm not mad. Not at all. That kiss was incredibly beautiful and I'm glad it happened. What could have happened afterward isn't meant to happen for us yet, if ever. You have no reason to be upset. I'm not."

"You promise?" she asks as she lifts her eyes to his again.

Wiping a tear that escapes her eye, he replies, "I promise. Things are happening fast between us. For most people this would take months and months, but for some reason, for us, it's happening now. We will take it slow, as slow as we can, and if it's meant to happen it will."

Leaning into him and letting herself be enveloped in his arms, she says, "Thank you."

They remain that way for a long time without a single word. Nothing needs to be said and when they separate, they say goodnight and that they will see each other in the morning.

***

Trinity

Trinity goes straight to the bathroom for a bubble bath. Once she is hidden by a tub full of hot water and bubbles, she begins to feel better about everything. She allows herself to sink low enough where all that is showing is her face. The bubbles fill the tub, covering her and the water.

Sheeba sits beside the tub with her chin resting on the edge, watching her and looking like she is about to jump in.

"Don't you even think about it, girl," Trinity giggles, trying to sound tough. "I'll give you one tomorrow."

Sheeba huffs at her and lays down beside the tub.

Trinity rests her head against the wall and takes deep breaths, thinking. She doesn't regret what happened. That kiss…their very first one…was incredible. She felt sparks from his lips like she had never felt before in her life.

That's what terrified her and she had to pull away. She thinks if she hadn't she would have allowed things to go a lot further. As a Christian she can't let that happen, but she hopes he will hold her and kiss her many more times. They will have to be careful.

***

David Tremper

David Tremper hasn't been able to find any kind of paper trail following Trinity. No transactions or withdrawals of any kind in her name. Obviously, she's smart enough to know better than to take money out from a machine. She hasn't paid for anything with a card either, so she has cash on her or someone is helping her. The detective sits back from his desk and thinks about calling Derrick to let him know that so far it's been a dry run, no luck at all on his precious girlfriend. It's been a month since Derrick hired him, and if Trinity does have cash, it will run out soon.

Tapping his pencil on the desk, he goes through the facts so far. He knows Trinity is originally from North Carolina, but moved to Connecticut from Colorado. He knows she has family down south, but from what her boyfriend told him they aren't close, so he doubts she's with any of them. He has a gut feeling she is with someone else. Someone who can help her on a much larger scale, but who?

Looking at the picture her boyfriend gave him he grins. Yeah, she's a pretty thing, all right. Why would she run? Why would she up and disappear for no reason? He has a strange gnawing instinct that Derrick, the jerk, didn't tell him everything there is to know. He probably smacked her around and she got tired of it; maybe she was even scared for her life. David hates guys like that, but it isn't his business. He's being paid to find out where she is. When he finds her, his business is done.

Logging onto his computer, he types in "Litchfield County" and the night she disappeared. He looks for any kind of accidents or arrests, but there isn't anything helpful to him. She isn't in any of the hospitals or shelters, either. He looks at the outgoing flights at all the airports, but again, there isn't anything with her name attached to it. Nothing at the bus stops, either. She doesn't have a car with her and she hasn't leased one, at least not in her real name.

She didn't just up and disappear into thin air, but it looks that way. The last thing he can look at before having to actually hit the streets are the recorded videos of the parking lot from that rainy night she ran. He doubts anything will turn up there either, but he needs to check that lead out.

Chapter Nine

Trinity

Trinity's Sunday morning begins with Sheeba licking her face…again. She giggles and lovingly pushes her away, telling her to stop.

"Good morning to you too, you big love bug."

Panting and drooling on the blanket, Sheeba rests her front legs on Trinity's chest and doesn't move until she receives a long scratch on her head and behind her ears. Trinity has to make her move by sitting up and removing the covers.

"Sorry girl, but I have got to get ready for church. I know you understand, of course."

Sheeba barks and rests her furry chin on Trinity's pillow as she watches her kneel and pray, follows her into the bathroom, then into the kitchen. Gates is already awake and at the table with the morning paper and coffee. He looks up at her and smiles the second he sees her.

"Good morning."

Glad to see him already awake she grins back at him. Feeling wonderful she replies, "Good morning to you too. Thanks for making coffee. How long have you been awake?"

"About an hour. I woke up for some reason and was wide awake, so I didn't see any reason to stay there. Besides, I have to get ready soon."

"Oh? You going somewhere this morning."

He lays the paper down and presses his lips. "Yeah, I was thinking last night about something. Something important."

Sitting down across from him with her cup, a curious grin, and hair astray she asks, "And what might that be?"

"I was thinking about going to church with you today. If that's okay."

Her eyes bulge and she almost spits out her coffee onto the table in surprise.

"Really? Well, yeah, of course it's okay. I would love for you to go with me. What brought that on?"

Shrugging his shoulders, he says, "I don't know, to be honest. It entered my mind last night as I was thinking about you and how you said going to church made so many great changes in how you feel so quickly. Also, I was thinking more about the nightmare I recently had and when I woke up it was still on my mind, so I sort of want to check it out."

"Soooo, you aren't going just to impress me?" she asks suspiciously.

"No, of course not," he laughs. "I mean, in a small way it is because of you, but no I'm not going to make you like me more. I really do want to go. Trust me when I say it surprises me too."

"Well, in that case you made my heart smile. I'm thrilled you want to go."

They stare and smile at each other for a few seconds and it's obvious last night means something to both of them, but don't bring it up. Instead, they talk about eating a small breakfast and getting ready. It doesn't take long, but they realize they need to hurry if they want make it on time.

An hour later they are stepping out of the car, walking toward the church door and she feels the need to hold his hand. When their fingers intertwine they both smile and walk in together.

***

Gates

It's the first time in years Gates has stepped inside a church. Everyone he meets makes him feel as if he is part of the family, and he starts to understand why Trinity feels so good about this place. As they walk down between the pews he looks around at the architecture and is impressed. He particularly likes the large mural of the Last Supper behind the pulpit, where the baptisms are given.

Trinity tugs on his hand and they sit near the front of the church as the choir begins to walk onto the stage. His emotions surprise him when they start singing, and he even sings a little with the congregation. He doesn't have a Bible and notices Trinity doesn't either. He will have to make sure she gets one. Maybe after they leave they can go to

Walmart or somewhere and buy one for her. He knows she will like that.

After two songs and the offering, the pastor begins his sermon. Gates listens to the pastor talk about the faith of a mustard seed and how if someone has at least that much, anything is possible. It confuses him a little, but he enjoys it. When they say goodbye and get back in the car, Trinity asks him what he thinks.

"I didn't completely understand the sermon, but I did enjoy being here. I'm glad I came with you."

Smiling and leaning against him, she slides her arm within his. "I'm glad too."

The fact she is being openly affectionate brings up confused feelings, but he doesn't complain. He loves the way she feels against him. When they leave the parking lot he tells her they are going to Walmart first, then get some lunch before going home.

When they reach the city limits of Bedford, they witness a horrible car accident. Since they are the first people who stop to help, their unplanned adventure of the day brings something else they didn't expect. Fortunately, the collision isn't fatal to those involved, but news crews show up. Both Gates and Trinity are caught on camera as the police talk with them.

***

David Tremper

Someone in Connecticut is watching the national

news that afternoon as he sits on the sofa, eating lunch and drinking a beer. He smiles broadly when he sees the beautiful young black lady standing helplessly to the side, oblivious to the fact she has been found. The detective immediately writes the information down and tells himself that once in a blue moon his job is very easy. His job is finished as far as he is concerned. All he has to do is make a phone call.

***

Gates

"I hope that couple will be okay," Trinity says during the drive to Walmart. "They looked pretty shaken up."

Gates has a stern look on his face when he answers. "I'm sure they are going to be fine. They're in good hands now. The hardest part for them will be getting the insurance and car taken care of."

"Are you okay?" she asks. She can hear something different in his tone and knows something isn't right.

He looks at her and lies, faking a smile. "Huh? Oh, yeah I'm fine. Just thinking about something is all." He doesn't want to worry her by telling her the truth. He saw the cameras and the reporters, and has a bad feeling about them being on the news. Even though they weren't interviewed by the media, he knows they were caught on film. If her boyfriend sees her on the news, it won't be long before there is trouble. Not long at all.

Nothing more is said about it. They walk into Walmart and he takes her to the book section to pick out a Bible she likes. The act of generosity from him brings pure joy to her and in the aisle, in front of the books, she hugs him and gives him a small kiss.

"Thank you, you are so sweet to me. I don't deserve this at all."

"You're welcome and of course you do. How do you like this one?" he reaches down and picks up a leather bound King James Version.

Trinity takes it from him and holds it to her chest.

"It's perfect," she softly replies with a tear in her eye.

"Okay, I will get this one," he comments and takes a black one from the shelf. "So we don't get them mixed up."

Laughing, she holds his hand and they walk up front to pay. They eat lunch at the Subtrak inside Walmart before they go home. He can't get the nagging feeling of trouble out of his thoughts, but hides it well. He knows he will have to take some precautions, but he can't say anything to her yet. He can't keep it from her for long because she needs to be ready in case anything does happen. He'll think about it more before talking to her.

***

Later that evening, Gates takes the locked safe from beneath his bed and sets it on the dresser.

Unlocking it, he looks at what lies within—something he hasn't had to use in years and he hopes he won't have to for a very long time. Unfortunately, he has a feeling he may not have a choice. Removing the SIG SAUER P226 from the safe, he's immediately swarmed with memories he doesn't like. Turning it over in his hands, he knows that even though he hasn't used it in a while, he will never forget how. He's had more than enough rounds leave the barrel on this baby. He takes the time to make sure it's clean and loaded before setting it beneath his pillow. He has to be prepared for anything now. He has to keep Trinity safe under all circumstances.

***

Derrick

"You are one hundred percent certain that it's her?" Derrick asks the detective over the phone.

"Totally, one hundred percent, yes. I have her picture and I watched the news clip several times before I called you. I even recorded it to make sure. It's her all right."

"Okay, thanks. The rest of your money will be in the bank by the end of the hour."

Derrick ends the call he wasn't actually expecting so soon. He figured it would take a little longer, but he's not complaining. He's thrilled, but surprised. Moneta, Virginia? Who does she know down there? It doesn't matter. He knows where she is now, or at least the general area. She will be so surprised when she sees him. He laughs out loud when he imagines the look that will be on her face.

"Sweetheart, you will be coming home soon to be with Daddy, whether you like it or not. You should know better than to run from me."

He picks up the picture of them together that was taken during the spring. He stares at it for a long moment then throws it in the trash. He has plans and logs onto the computer to start making them happen.

Chapter Ten

Gates

"I don't understand why I can't go find a job. I'm tired of being stuck in the house." Trinity is doing her best to control her temper as she glares at Gates. "Explain to me why you think it's best that I don't. Come on, I want to hear it."

Gates frowns and squeezes his hands until his knuckles turn white. He doesn't like her tone, but he can see the frustration all over her face and can certainly hear it in her voice. He knows she should be able to work, and he understands her being upset. She's been living in his house for close to a month and a half, and if the roles were switched he would feel the same way or worse. He has no choice but to be honest with her.

"You remember last Sunday when I went to church with you?" he asks as he looks into her beautiful, angry eyes.

"Yes; what does that have to do with anything?"

"Afterward, when we witnessed that accident and the cameras were all around us, did you see them? We were on the news even though we didn't talk to anyone in the media."

Her expression immediately changed and she asks with a higher tone in her voice, "Are you sure? You saw us on the news?"

He nods. "I did. I watched the news that night, but I didn't say anything about it because I didn't want to worry you. This has been on my mind ever since."

She lowers her gaze to the table as if she isn't sure what to say. "What, exactly, does this mean?"

"It means if your boyfriend, or anyone else you know was watching, there's a chance they saw you. That means they know you are in or near Moneta."

She sighs heavily and rests her face in her palms. Fear creeps up her spine and into her heart. Neither of them speaks for a few seconds, but he finally asks if she's okay.

"I don't know...I don't know. I understand what you mean now, I think. I'm sorry I got so upset with you."

"You are here for me to help you, Trinity. It's my responsibility to protect you."

She still isn't able to say a word. As he speaks, he can see her shoulders begin to tremble as her emotions take over. He stands and takes her in his arms, holding her as she cries into his shoulder. Fear of Derrick finding her and what may happen if he does probably consumes her.

She remains in Gates' arms until she can breathe and regain control of herself.

He holds her at arms' length, lifts her face to look at her, and says, "I will not let anything happen to you. You are more than just someone I am helping. You have become so much more to me than that. Do you trust me?"

She nods, telling him she does. She sniffs and takes a deep breath, and her eyes rest on his again. Without warning, she stands on her toes, leans into him, wraps her arms around his neck and presses her lips against his. Surprised, but more than willing, he pulls her into his embrace and takes her lips with passion. He can tell she wants to be with him and he certainly knows he wants her, but how far can they let it go? He doesn't want to push her for anything she isn't willing to do. Their lips are locked together and the world outside of them disappears. Their body heat rises rapidly and once again they separate before they can't stop. This time it's Gates who pulls back first.

He closes his eyes, breathing hard, and steps back. He can hear Trinity sigh out loud. "I had to stop," he tells her quickly. "I didn't want too, but I had to."

She takes his hand in hers and says, "I know, it was getting…intense. I'm sorry." She leans into his arms again without another word.

He holds her and can feel his heart hammering. "Never, ever say you are sorry for what just happened. I'm not sorry." A moment passes and he steps back, leaning against the counter still holding her hand. With his other hand he runs his fingers through his hair and shakes his head.

"What's happening here, Trinity?"

"What do you mean? Between us?"

"Yes. When I picked you up from Howard and Mattie's, neither of us thought for a second anything like this would happen. Now look at us, barely able to control ourselves. Don't get me wrong—I'm certainly not complaining."

Unable to look away or lie to him, she whispers, "I know it's getting really difficult and it does kind of sound like you are complaining, but I know you aren't."

"My feelings for you have grown deep, Trinity."

"I feel the same way. Honestly, I'm worried."

"About what? I mean other than what might happen with your ex."

She steps back, biting her bottom lip and sits at the table with a serious look. Folding her arms, she stares at Sheeba who is lying a few feet away, staring back with her sad eyes and thumping her tail on the floor.

"I need to do some serious praying...about everything. About Derrick possibly coming here. About what's happening between us and the Christian I am supposed to be. I want to live like I believe Jesus wants me to. I truly do, and please don't take this the wrong way, but we are quickly getting into a situation that is very tempting and difficult."

"I'm not taking it the wrong way. I know how difficult it is. I support you with your faith and since I went to church with you, I've been thinking about it a lot myself."

"You have?" She looks up at him.

"Yeah, and it's weird in a way. I mean, I've

always known there's a higher power of sorts, and I guess I've always believed there's a God. I also have always had a hard time having faith or trying to live for someone I can't even see or talk to, especially with all I saw overseas. Some things in life make it hard to understand so much about religion. All of the insanity and misery in the world—I think a lot of that held me back for a long time."

"I know that pain, at least some of it, but I want you to ask yourself something."

"Okay, I'll try."

"How many times when you were deployed while on active duty did you face death? How many times do you think you should have been killed, but instead you are sitting here with me?"

Looking deep into her eyes he answers, "More times than I care to think about."

"Do you think you are alive today because God wanted you to be here for some reason?"

He thinks about what she's asking him and rubs his eyes. He wants to believe that's why he is still here, that God wants him here. Maybe God has always had a plan for him. Maybe he is supposed to be here helping women in need, or more specifically, helping Trinity. He's not sure, but he's beginning to think there's definitely a God upstairs loving him, even though he feels he doesn't deserve that love.

"You know what, Trinity? There's a lot I don't understand or know, but I do know that I'm tired of going through life wondering and not being sure why I'm here. I'm tired of thinking God is up there wanting the best for me, and me not doing whatever it is I'm supposed to be doing with my life."

"Maybe you are doing some of it right now by being here for me."

"Maybe, yeah, I thought about that, but I think…no, I know I want to keep going to church with you. If you want to, I would also like to start reading the Bible with you. Maybe I will learn and understand things better that way."

***

Trinity

She can't believe what she hears; her heart swells and her smile widens. "I would love that so much."

"I wonder too…" he stops, unsure if he should finish what he wants to say.

"What? What are you wondering?"

"Do you think God put you here with me for more than your protection?"

She thinks about what he's asking, and hopes with all her heart that he's right. Even though she has been in his life for only a short time, she is falling for him.

"Yes," she whispers. "I think He put us together for more than that. I think there's a very good chance God wants us to be together to love each other. I'm really beginning to believe that."

Smiling, he tenderly holds her hand, lifts it to his lips and kisses the back of it. "I'm beginning to believe that too."

She gets up from her chair and leaves the room, telling him she'll be right back. Confused, he sits there wondering what she's up to. A moment later she returns and sits beside him, holding both Bibles.

"Why don't we start with a prayer?" They smile, hold hands and close their eyes.

***

Derrick

Derrick doesn't think it will be difficult to bring Trinity home where she belongs. He doesn't know her exact location, but he will find her easily enough. From what he found on Google, Moneta, Virginia is a small country town. He feels she had to have been seen enough that if he shows her picture around he will be able to find her. He also thinks she's probably staying with someone because she hasn't touched her money in the bank the entire time she's been gone. Someone has to be helping her. Whoever that person is will do one of two things. They will either believe the lies he will tell about Trinity—that she is mentally unstable and he needs to look after her—or they will regret getting involved. He doesn't want to hurt anyone; he only wants the woman he loves to be with him. In the end, when this is all over, he believes she will be.

Derrick finishes packing a small suitcase with clothes and toiletries. He picks up the handgun he hopes he won't have to use. He has to admit though, it looks and feels great in his hands. A lightweight 9mm he purchased the day after Trinity decided to

114

run off. He was still pretty upset at the time, otherwise he probably wouldn't have bought it. Since he knows where she is he's calmed down, but he is going to take it just in case matters turn down a different path than he wants them to go.

Tonight, he will rest and get mentally ready for what is waiting for him. Will it turn out to be violent? He doesn't know, but he's ready for that if it comes down to it. The one thing he really doesn't like about walking into this is that he has no idea who is helping Trinity. It could be a man or a woman. If her friend is a man, is he dangerous? Not knowing anything about the person bothers him, but he can take care of business either way. The less drama the better. He will just have to wait and see what goes down.

Chapter Eleven

Trinity

Her dream flirts with her as a scene of snow-capped mountains and pine trees passes gently through her mind. She sees soft and fluffy clouds above the tips of the far away peaks and her hair falls into her face as a breeze picks up. As she sits on the freshly cut grass and leans back onto her hands, she senses another presence and turns to see the form of a man approaching. Before she is able to see the face of the stranger or before either can speak, she hears a loud noise that breaks her away from the endearing moment.

Trinity jerks awake and opens her eyes to the sound of Sheeba snoring beside her, and she can't help but giggle. Sometimes she thinks her fur baby can sleep through anything. Trinity lies still for a while and thinks about how well she slept, which doesn't surprise her since her life is better now and with a lot less stress. She tries to focus on the interrupted dream, but already it has begun to fade away into oblivion.

Not long ago she would have been terrified, but for some reason she's only a little nervous. For that alone she is extremely grateful. She knows there is a lot to be grateful for. First and foremost, she has a loving and powerful God in her life, and He loves her enough to keep her safe and alive by putting her with Gates. They are getting very close, a lot closer than she would have ever imagined when they first met. She finds it completely amazing how fast things have happened in such a short time. She wouldn't change it for the world, not even the events that led up to their meeting. If all of those things hadn't happened she probably would have never met Gates. The way he makes her smile and the way he holds her, kisses her and wants her makes her want to be with him as well.

Suddenly, Sheeba raises her head and looks at her, panting. She sits up and leans forward, trying to give Trinity good morning kisses, making her laugh out loud.

"Good morning to you too, sweetie!" she says, closing her eyes and turning her head to avoid getting licked to death. She quickly gets out of bed to remove herself from the dog's loving attack and walks to the bathroom, Sheeba right behind her.

"Do you have to follow me everywhere?" she asks the dog as she relieves herself then brushes her teeth. Sheeba sits on her rump looking at her as if she should already know the answer to that question. "Right, of course you do. Come on, let's go outside."

Together they walk through the kitchen. Trinity can smell the coffee brewing and wonders where Gates is. When she takes Sheeba out, she sees him sitting on the back deck with his eyes closed and begins to worry if he's okay.

"Good morning," she greets him as Sheeba nudges his hand to see if he's awake. Opening his eyes he smiles at them both and rubs the dog's head, letting her know he is okay.

"Good morning, beautiful. How are you?"

His sweet greeting makes her smile. "I'm great. How are you this morning? You worried me for a second when I saw you out here with your eyes closed."

"Just doing some meditation while I was waiting for two things."

"What two things?" "Coffee and you."

She laughs at him for being cute and leans down to kiss him. Sheeba runs between them and out into the yard to do her business. They can hear the gurgling noises coming from the kitchen and go back inside for coffee. Before she can reach for a cup, Gates wraps his arms around her stomach and pulls her back into him. She smiles and allows him to hug her and rests her hands on his.

"I can't help but tell you that you are incredibly gorgeous when you first wake up," he whispers to her.

She laughs out loud at him. "You must need glasses, mister. I look terrible in the morning, my hair is a mess, and I don't have any make-up on, but thank you for your kind words."

He reaches for a cup for each of them. "I'll have you know that my eyesight is perfect 20/20 vision in both eyes. And I think you are a natural beauty and don't need make-up."

"Awww, well ain't you the sweetheart this morning," Trinity replies and kisses him on the cheek.

"Sometimes I try to be."

With their cups they walk back out onto the porch and watch Sheeba rolling around in the grass. There is a chill in the air, but it isn't too bad. Soon she knows it will be too cold to be outside so early in the morning sitting on the deck, and not long afterward winter will be upon them. They are enjoying it while they can. Out of the blue Trinity says something and catches him off guard.

"Thank you for last night. You have no idea how much that means to me."

"What? What did I do other than be honest about everything?"

"That's what I'm talking about. I'm not used to a man opening up to me like that. It really says a lot about you and it means the world to me. Thank you."

Staring out at the lake he takes a sip of his coffee. "Like I told you a couple of weeks ago, I've grown a lot since I've lived here. Meditation, being with nature, the quietness and exercise, and Tai Chi have really helped me come a long way. Honesty with myself is a part of it. Oh, that reminds me, since we are talking about honesty. It appears to me that laziness has crept upon us as of late."

She mocks being hurt from being called lazy and

playfully slaps his arm.

"Who are you calling lazy?"

He laughs, holds up a hand in defense and says, "Just saying that the past couple of days we haven't done much as far as workouts go. Not pointing any fingers at you; it's my fault too." They grin at each other and he continues. "To stay with the honesty thing, I also thank you for last night. Well, for everything actually."

"What have I done?"

He looks at his cup and runs a finger around the rim. "You are a big part of the reason my eyes have been opened. With you here, I see a better meaning for my life, possibly why I'm still around."

She can't help but smile. She leans forward and reaches for his hand. "Thank you, that means a lot. I think there's a reason for everything."

"I agree."

They sit at the table and she starts to think about making a real breakfast when she gets another shock from him.

"How would you feel about meeting a friend of mine?"

"You have friends around here?"

He laughs and asks, "Why? Does that surprise you?"

"I'm sorry that didn't sound right. I only meant that you haven't mentioned anyone other than when you told me you have some secret friends, but you weren't telling me anything about them."

"Yeah, I know, but I do have one friend who lives in Lynchburg. It's about an hour's drive, but I haven't seen her in a while and I think you would like her. I know she would love you."

"Okay, then. I would love to meet her."

Nodding with a grin he says, "I'll call her in a while then, once we get a few things done. We should workout and eat before we do anything else."

"I was thinking about making a real breakfast, but let's get the workout out of the way, shower, then I'll cook us something."

"Sounds like a plan. Let's do it."

They change into something more fitting to break a sweat in and proceed to the basement. It doesn't take long before they both have sweat streaming down their backs and are breathing hard. They manage to complete a decent amount of time on the machines and even work in a small Tai Chi routine. They are tired by the time they go back upstairs, except for Sheeba. She wants to play.

***

Derrick

On the highway, Derrick curses the drivers around him, calling them all sorts of names. He can't figure out why so many people are given the privilege of drivers' licenses. He is doing his best to not let them affect his main goal—to get to Virginia in a timely manner, unscathed and without getting pulled over. The last thing he wants or needs is to get in trouble for having a firearm in his possession. He doesn't have a permit for a concealed weapon, so being questioned about it by a cop will not be a good idea.

It's starting to get dark and he still has a way to go before he arrives at the Virginia state line. All he can think about is finding Trinity. Even though he's angry for her running away from him, he still misses everything about her. He knows he has an anger problem and when he sees her, he'll promise to get help. He knows a man shouldn't hit a woman, but with the life he grew up with, watching his father beat his mother and getting abused himself most of his life, it sort of made him who he is.

Still, it's no excuse and he knows that. He is angry at himself for how bad things got. He wants her back. No…he needs her back. He needs to make things right again, if she will let him. If not, he will make her see it his way. Even though he is willing to get help he will still make sure she sees things his way. That's what his father always told him—that the woman has her place in a relationship and it is behind her man. For some reason he can't make her see that. She will either be with him or she won't be with anyone…ever.

He thinks about her eyes and how they sparkle when she smiles. Oh, and her smile, how beautiful it is. He misses seeing her when she's happy and laughing. She's definitely a rose that stands out in the middle of everyone else. He's miserable without her. He is willing to go to prison over her if it comes down to it.

***

Gates

"I talked to my friend while you were in the shower, and she said she would love to meet you," Gates tells Trinity when she walks into the kitchen that evening. The day flew by and they have enjoyed it the best that they can. After they had their workout, took showers, and had breakfast they read from the Bible. He had plenty of questions for her to answer.

"Fantastic! When will we be going?"

"She offered to cook dinner for us tomorrow night. She said to be there around seven."

"Sounds good to me, and what's her name? You forgot to mention that."

"Oh, sorry, her name's Katherine."

"Care to tell me a little about her?" she asks, sitting cross-legged in the chair opposite him.

He leans on his forearms and tries not to focus on how incredibly gorgeous she is, fresh out of the shower. She's wearing her pajamas and has her hair wrapped in a towel. She'd think she isn't anywhere close to being beautiful, but to him she always is. He composes himself as best he can and begins to tell her about Katherine.

"Do you remember me telling you about helping another woman a couple of years ago?" "So that's her?"

"Yeah, that's her and we still talk once in a while. Not a lot, but she likes to keep me up to date on how she's doing. Thankfully, her life is much better than it used to be. She's very smart and a compassionate person. It was a real mess what she had to go through. A lot like what happened to you, only she's marked for life."

"What do you mean?"

"The guy she had to get away from was sick in the head. He held her down one night when he was drunk and held a burning stick from the fireplace to her face, injuring her badly. Even with surgery it didn't completely remove her scars, and she lost the sight in her left eye because of it."

Trinity gapes in horror at what Katherine went through, and holds her hand over her mouth. "Where is he? I hope he's in prison for what he did to her."

"He spent some time in jail for it, but basically all he got was a slap on the wrist. By the time I met her she was more than just afraid for her life. Anyhow, not too long after she came to me, his threat to her ended when he ran his mouth to the wrong people at a bar one night and someone shot him. He died on the way to the hospital."

She doesn't know what to say. She shakes her head at the horror she can so easily and unfortunately relate to.

"By the grace of God it didn't go that far with me. I truly have compassion for the poor woman."

"Like I said, you'll like her and I have no doubt she will like you, too."

"I look forward to meeting her, and I bet we will have a lot to talk about. But right now, I think it's your turn to fix dinner." She claps her hands and rubs them together. "So, what's on the menu?"

They laugh and he shrugs, having no clue since he hasn't thought about it. Looking through the cabinets he feigns confusion. She gives him a hard time by jabbing him in his side and points out the pasta and sauce in the cabinets and the ingredients for a salad in the refrigerator, but he uses the idea of Chinese take-out.

"You are so lucky right now," she says with a touch of sarcasm and crosses her arms, trying to look mad but failing miserably.

Grinning from ear to ear, he asks, "Why am I so lucky?"

"Three reasons. One, I love Chinese food. Two, I happen to be falling for you. And three, because I don't want to hear you whining."

He laughs loudly and grabs her, pulling her against him. "You're falling for me, huh?" Her heart beats furiously in her chest. Her eyes meet his and her voice becomes a whisper. "Oh, yes...without a doubt."

"That's a good thing," he replies and tightens his hold as he lowers his mouth to hers. "Because I'm falling hard for you, too."

Their lips touch and the room spins around them as they get lost in each other's embrace. Once again they find themselves wanting and needing the other more than air, but it comes to an end when Sheeba pushes her way between them, barking loudly, interrupting the moment.

"I'll take that as a sign," Trinity says as she leans against the counter to catch her breath.

"Yeah, probably a good thing. Go ahead and get dressed and get your jacket, and I'll feed her. Then we'll go."

"Okay, I'll be right back."

"Come on, girl," he says to the dog. "I know you love her more than me, but I'm feeding you tonight."

He watches the dog look down the hall after Trinity; he can hear her laughing as she goes.

Chapter Twelve

Trinity

Katherine is waiting for them when they arrive, and opens the door before they have a chance to knock. She's thrilled to see them and wraps her slender arms around them in excitement.

"Oh, it's so good to see you! I've missed you!" she exclaims as she squeezes Gates.

"It's great to see you, too. This is Trinity." He introduces them and steps to the side.

"Well, hey there, it's great to meet you," Katherine says.

"Thank you, its great meeting you as well." She sees what Gates mentioned to her even though she tries not to stare. The scar isn't hideous, but it's definitely noticeable.

"Y'all come inside and let me get you something to drink. Would you like me to make some coffee?"

"Sure, that would be nice. Do you want any help?" Trinity offers.

127

"You are my guest, so you two just have a seat. It'll only take a few minutes."

They follow Katherine and sit at the kitchen table. Trinity observes the small area and loves how it is decorated. She has a small apartment, but comfortable. She notices the religious magnets on the refrigerator and a plaque hanging on the wall that reads *As for me and my house, we will serve the Lord*. Smiling, she knows she likes Katherine already.

"So tell me Trinity, if you don't mind, are you from this area? Or have you recently had to come here from somewhere else to get away?"

Trinity looks at Gates and he shrugs, so she figures she may as well be open, at least about some of it since Katherine has been through so much herself.

"I, umm, well I guess you could say I had to come here from Connecticut to get away from someone."

"I hope you don't mind me asking, but I sort of figured it was something along those lines since you are with Gates. I didn't know where from, though. He only told me he was bringing a friend with him he thought I would like to meet."

"He surprised me with the idea too, but to be able to meet someone else he has helped means a lot."

Katherine sits with them. "Did he tell you anything about me?"

Trinity takes a nervous breath and answers. "He did. I hope you don't mind."

Gates looks back and forth between the two

ladies as they talk as if he isn't there. Katherine looks at him and reaches for his hand.

"Gates was a Godsend for me. I'm glad he told you and I'm glad you both are here. It hasn't been easy to get through what happened, but since…it has gotten somewhat easier. I truly believe Gates is an angel, but he always finds that funny when I say it."

He laughs lightly at Katherine's comment. "I wouldn't go so far as to say I'm an angel on any level. I will say, though, that I believe we were put in each other's lives at the right time for a reason. The same goes for Trinity."

The atmosphere is grounded with deep discussion about what happened to them as both Katherine and Trinity get to know one another. Gates sits patiently and listens, allowing them to have their girl talk—no judgements, only total honesty and relating.

"I met Gates a day after I ran away from my abusive boyfriend. He brought me down here from Connecticut and I've been here a little over a month now. Things have been a huge adjustment as far as the exercise routines, not being able to work, and not being able to touch my money in the bank, but I'm safe and things have improved on certain levels."

***

Katherine

Katherine sees Trinity look at Gates when she

speaks of him. She catches the sparkle in her eyes, and from his smile she knows there's something special taking place between the two of them. She doesn't say anything about it, but lets Trinity do the talking.

"My boyfriend, or I should say my ex-boyfriend, was very controlling and seemed to enjoy hitting me. It got so bad I was afraid for my life. The night I finally had the courage to run I will never be able to forget. We had gone to a bar and I really didn't want to be there. When he went to the backroom to do some type of business, I knew it was my only chance. The weather was horrible—it was pouring rain, but I didn't care. I only had a few minutes and I made the best of it. I found an unlocked car and hid in it. Thankfully there wasn't a lot of lighting around. I was taking a huge chance hiding in a stranger's car. I will forever believe that God made sure I would be safe because it turned out to be a pastor's wife's car. She had seen me get in and heard him walking around yelling for me. When she got in the car she didn't say anything until we drove away, then took me to her house. They gave me a safe place to sleep that night and called Gates to help me. I will be eternally grateful for them."

Katherine nods and replies, "It seems we have a lot in common. Can I assume that the pastor's wife is Mattie and the pastor is Howard?"

"Yeah," Trinity answers with a grin. "Another pair of angels that obviously God sent to help us both. Unfortunately, in some ways we do have a lot in common. Depending on how we look at it though, it all turned out to be good."

"It's been a blessing in certain ways as well for me," Katherine tells them. "With all of the horrible things that happened, with all of the pain and misery I lived through, I have to say the best thing that came out of it was that I found God. Today, I am happier than I've ever been. I truly feel blessed, and I love Howard and Mattie. I miss them."

Gates looks at Katherine and smiles as Trinity comments. "I know what you mean. I've always believed in God. I used to go to church, but Derrick didn't like it and would get upset about me going so I stopped. Now, though, I am going again and found a church I like. I have rededicated myself to Jesus. I'm trying hard to have faith that this will all get better somehow. I don't know how, but I'm trying to believe."

Katherine looks at Gates suddenly and asks, "Are you going to just sit there and let us do all the talking?"

He laughs. "I'm letting the two of you get acquainted, and I'm still not completely sure about the whole God thing yet. I did go to church with her last time, though."

"Oh, really? Well that's a shocker."

"I'm surprised too, to be honest," he tells her.

She places their cups on the table and grins. "It wouldn't have anything to do with being attracted to her, would it?"

He blushes; they see his face turning red and giggle. Trinity places her hand on his arm as he answers.

"Ummm, yeah I have to admit that's part of it, but not totally. I'm curious, I'll say that much.

Honestly, when I went I found it very humbling and educational. I mean, in a way it was confusing, but I want to go again. I feel there's a purpose for me and part of it could be going to church. I don't know yet though."

"I would rather you be going out of curiosity than not at all. I will not pressure you about any of it. This is something between you and God. Only you can live for Him if and when you want to and are ready," Trinity tells him as she looks him square in the eyes.

"Thank you, I appreciate that."

***

Gates

The conversation drifts toward what happened last Sunday and the feeling he has about being on camera. "I believe the man she ran from is searching for her, and I fear someone Trinity knows, if not Derrick himself, saw the news that day."

"What will you do if he shows up?" Katherine asks.

"Whatever I have to do to protect her, but hopefully it won't come down to that." He looks at Trinity and holds her hand. Nothing more is said about it.

The conversation turns to what Katherine has been doing lately and she tells them about her job, her newest hobby, and a secret she has been holding onto for a couple of weeks. She tells them about a guy she met at church who asked her out for dinner. She is actually thinking about going.

"I'll have to get back to you on that," she jokes.

Their evening visiting with one another passes too fast as they enjoy the conversation and the dinner Katherine prepares. Before they know it, it's time for Trinity and Gates to get back to the cabin. Hugging before they leave, they promise to make plans in the near future for some fun.

***

When they get home that evening, Trinity says she is going to take a bubble bath. Gates rests on the couch in the living room with Sheeba and watches television. He feels good about how the evening went with Katherine. The girls became instant friends and he's happy about how easily the two of them connected. He knows them both well enough to know they need each other in their lives.

He runs his fingers through Sheeba's thickening fur as she lies next to him, a rare occurrence. Once Trinity comes in the room, Sheeba will be with her and he will no longer exist. It's nice having her next to him, even if only for a few minutes. As he scratches her neck, he thinks about Trinity's boyfriend and what it might be like to face him. She has described him, and by what she says Gates thinks he is most likely a big, cowardly bully. Gates handled a lot tougher and stronger men while he was in the service. He isn't very concerned about Derrick's physical strength, but he does worry about Derrick's intelligence. How ruthless will he be to get her back? That's what worries him. *Will Derrick be able to sneak up and get a hold of Trinity before I can protect her?* No; he can't allow that to happen. Even if he wasn't falling in love with her, his priority is her safety. He has to keep her safe. He doesn't know why exactly, but he has an extremely strong feeling in his gut that something will happen soon. He learned years ago to trust that feeling. It is almost never wrong.

Suddenly, Sheeba jumps off the sofa, breaking his train of thought. He watches her pace to the bathroom door as it opens, and the woman he has sworn to protect steps out in her robe. He can't help staring at her. Trinity's skin still glistens from her bath and she looks like a goddess, the most incredibly beautiful woman he has ever seen. Gates knows now that he's madly in love with her. He isn't falling anymore. He has fallen, and fallen hard.

He knows if it comes down to it, he will give his life for her. He has no doubt about that. She reaches down and rubs Sheeba's head and turns to look at him. When she sees him staring at her she smiles and blows him a kiss. His heart jumps when the imaginary kiss hits him upside his head. He can only grin like a teenager watching the head cheerleader at a homecoming game, totally blindsided by her beauty.

"Are you okay?" she asks him with a slight hint of a whisper.

He barely hears her, but answers anyway. "I couldn't be better."

She giggles. "Okay. I'm going to go put on a nightgown and I'll be right back."

He mumbles "Okay" and watches her turn away.

"God, if you are up there, if you are real like Trinity says you are, please help me." He talks softly with his head laid back and his eyes closed. "If You really are listening to me, then You know what is happening. I don't know why You allow things like that to happen to people like Trinity, but we need Your help. I need to keep her safe. I love her and I can't lose her. Please help me, and God. One more thing. If You can find the time when this is all over down here, can you please help me... You know, make her happy. Amen."

A few minutes later Trinity walks into the living room in her nightgown and robe with Sheeba right beside her. She's still grinning and Gates gazes at her as if he's drugged. He wants to hold her, to kiss her, and badly wants to take her to bed and make love to her, but he will never push himself on her. If he ever has the honor and privilege of her giving herself to him, it will be on her terms. He'll just suffer in silence.

Trinity snuggles against him and he can smell the fragrance of her shampoo and body wash. He breathes in deeply, relishing her scent. He has to get a grip before he loses his mind. He places his arm around her and holds her close, enjoying every single second he has with her before things get crazy. They talk about their dinner with Katherine, and Gates asks what she thought.

"Oh, you were right, I absolutely adore her. Thank you for taking me there."

"You're welcome. It did look like you two hit it off fairly quick."

"Yeah, we did, right? She's a great cook, too. I loved her beef stew and biscuits. I could eat more right now!"

He laughs and says, "It's a good thing she sent some home with us, then."

"Nah, it's too late to be eating," she comments and burrows her face into his shoulder.

"Besides, I'm tired and think I'm going to bed in a few minutes."

He isn't tired at all anymore. Trinity nestled against him like she is does the total opposite of making him tired.

"Even though I can relate to some of her feelings and what she went through, I really feel sorry for her," Trinity says. "But at the same time I admire her strength and faith in God. She has moved forward with her life. It speaks volumes about her. Thank you again for taking me there tonight."

"You're welcome. I think she feels the same about you. I think you have made a lifelong friend."

"I think so too. I can use another one, that's for sure."

Gates holds her against him, too many feelings coursing through him at the same time. He caresses her arm and says, "I think I'm going to take a shower before bed." It will be a cold shower, but he doesn't say that.

Her hand slides around his stomach until her arm is all the way around him. She hugs him tightly, and he can feel the heat of her breath. Gates wonders if she has any idea what she is doing to him. He caresses her shoulder and kisses the top of her still damp head; neither of them say anything as they hold onto each other. Neither want to let go. After a few minutes Sheeba lets them know it's her turn to get some of the loving. She places her paws on their legs and huffs, making them laugh.

"I think someone is jealous," Trinity says.

"I think you're right."

"Oh, you poor deprived baby!" Trinity coos as she blows kisses to Sheeba and rubs her head. The sudden attention gets the dog excited and she starts prancing, making them laugh harder.

"I'm going for that shower now," Gates says as he starts to stand. Trinity quickly tightens her grip around him and plants a quick kiss before he has the chance to get away. He smiles and kisses her back, making it quick. Not going soon may lead to something he won't be able to stop. Trinity knows his predicament, and with a gleam in her eyes she lets him go.

"Enjoy your shower."

Laughing, he replies "I will."

***

Trinity

Trinity lies down on the couch and closes her eyes, knowing she should go to bed, but thoughts of Gates bounce around in her head. The temptation to be with him is attacking her and she struggles. It has been a long time since she's felt what she feels now. She loves these feelings for him, but knows she cannot act on them. The devil is playing with her soul and body, doing his best to weaken her so she falls into sins of the flesh. She isn't far from falling over the edge, but before she allows anything to happen she gets up, walks into her room, and falls to her knees, begging God to give her strength.

"Lord Jesus, my Heavenly Father, I know You are aware of my struggles. I know You are aware of all that is going on in my life and I love You for always being here for me. I need Your strength right now, Lord. Temptations are strong in me. I am weak and I need help. I believe You want me to be with Gates, but I also know You want things to be right. Please, help us Lord. Please, help us both walk the path You have for us. In Your name I pray, amen."

***

Gates

While Gates stands in the shower, he does his best to not think about his wants, about his overwhelming desire to be with the woman he has fallen for. He wants to show her his passion and feelings, but he also wants to respect her wishes and faith in the God she tries hard to live for. To do anything other than that would be wrong, and that's an understatement.

He leans forward with his hands on the walls of the shower and hangs his head, letting the water beat down on him. The water is as cold as he can stand it. He shivers, but it seems to be helping a little. He makes his mind go somewhere he isn't yet accustomed to, and he starts talking to the God he hopes is real and listening.

"God, I know only a few minutes ago I asked for Your help. Obviously, I will be asking for it a lot, but in the other room is a woman who has been put in my life for a reason. I know she's here for me to help her, but I'm thinking, too, that You brought her here for us to be together. I hope I'm not wrong about that. I haven't known her long, but she's so beautiful in every way that I couldn't help but fall in love. The last thing I want to do is hurt her by being a pig and pushing myself on her, so I'm begging You, if You are listening, please help me be strong for her."

He remains standing under the water with his eyes closed and tries to think of nothing, to clear his mind before finishing his shower. Instead of rushing to get out of the cold, he finally turns the heat up to almost blistering and relishes in the steam. Slowly he showers and once he's finished he feels confident enough to go to bed without any mishaps. He dries off, gets his robe on, and quickly walks into his room, shutting the door.

He doesn't hear anything from Trinity's room so he figures she's gone to bed. He wants to tell her goodnight, but slides between his own sheets instead. It's going to be a long night.

***

Derrick

Derrick isn't far from his destination, but his eyes have grown dangerously tired so he gets a room at a small hotel. As much as he wants to find Trinity and have her in his arms again, there's no real reason to be hasty. Lying on the bed he listens to the news without much interest. He has more important things on his mind. He is tired when he stops, but once he lies down his brain seems to say *Oh no you don't, you ain't going to sleep yet!*

Images run through his mind about the night she left. He remembers running through the rain, calling her name. He searched the parking lot and peered into cars, but didn't see her. He even tried opening a few of them, but they were all locked. He remembers picking up a large rock, seriously thinking about bashing in some of the windows. Thankfully some common sense showed up and stopped him. He didn't particularly want to go to jail, on that night or any other. He couldn't think of where she disappeared to so quickly. Maybe she planned it and had someone help her by meeting her outside, but he doubted it. He had enough of a hold on her so he knew all of her so-called friends. At least he thought he did.

He holds her picture in his hands and looks at her smile. God, she's beautiful. If she was with him right then he would be making love to her. He misses that part, too. He thinks about getting a prostitute, but decides he would be lowering his standards by doing that. No, he wants her and he will have her. The hardest part will be finding her.

He knows she's in Moneta, but he doesn't know exactly where. From what he found on Google it's a very small town, so someone has to have seen her. He decides to stop thinking about her and tries to get some sleep. He has a feeling he will have a long day ahead of him.

Chapter Thirteen

Derrick arrives in Moneta around nine o'clock and the traffic is light. Of course, it's a small country town and since it's Sunday morning, he doesn't expect to see a lot of people out and about. If he wasn't looking for her he would probably still be in bed himself. He drives around thinking about where to start looking. The image of her standing on the side of the road on the news makes him think about where she could have been that day. It had been a Sunday, and she was wearing a dress. He shakes his head and realizes the chance of her having been to church was very good. Did she go alone or with someone?

He doubts she was able to get herself a car since her name hasn't come up in any records of any kind. He also realizes that in this hick town, there are probably thousands of small roads. If he has to drive around, it can take a while.

Driving past an elementary school, he observes his surroundings and wonders why anyone would want to live where there is so little to do. What could be so great about living in such a horrendously boring place? He thinks about what kind of churches there would be in Moneta. Churches? Where would there be a church? There can only be a few of them, he thinks. He will find one and park, waiting to see if she shows up. First he needs a cup of coffee. When he sees a country store up ahead he slows and pulls into the gravel parking lot.

He slowly walks around the store, smirking at how simple and plain it looks. Compared to what he is used to there isn't much to offer, unless someone is fishing, hunting, or a junk food junkie. When he sees the small refrigerator holding nightcrawlers, he shakes his head and walks around, still looking for coffee. He is surprised they actually have a decent coffee bar near the back of the store. After paying, he returns to his car, thinking there is no possible way he could live somewhere like this.

He stays in the small gravel lot for a few more minutes, holding her picture and staring at it. His eyes are pained as he takes a long draw from his cigarette and blows a cloud of smoke through the cracked window. He realizes he should ask the cashier if anyone has seen her around. He throws the remaining unsmoked cigarette onto the gravel and walks back into the store.

"Excuse me. I was wondering if you have seen this lady around anytime recently?"

The woman behind the counter takes the picture. Over her glasses she looks at it and answers, "She's very pretty. I think I would remember her, but no, I can't say that I have. I'm sorry."

Nodding, Derrick takes the picture back, thanks her and walks out. He asks the guy who is walking in, but he gets the same response. Once he is in his car he shakes his head with frustration; someone has to have seen her. He will find her. It's just a matter of time. For now he will drive around, stop at a few places to show her picture around and ask the same questions. When he thinks church should be letting out, he will be sure to be sitting outside of one, watching for her.

He leaves the small store and takes a left where he sees a sign that reads Smith Mountain Lake. There should be some places around there where he can stop and ask about her. Probably some other stores and restaurants.

***

Gates

Both Trinity and Gates oversleep and have to rush around getting ready. They try not to run into each other in the process. Trinity has no intention of missing church and hearing the gospel. Gates wants to go mainly to make sure she will be safe, but with his struggles he knows being in the house of God certainly won't hurt him. While she is rushing around, he makes sure he sticks the SIG SAUER P226 in the back of his pants, nice and snug against his back. He hopes she won't notice he is carrying, and that he won't have to pull it out. He feels bad enough as it is about having it in church. He covers it with a sports jacket and walks out into the kitchen to wait for Trinity. They don't bother with breakfast; she takes Sheeba out to do her business then jumps in the car. They didn't even have time to get coffee, so on the way she says they still have a few minutes and asks him to stop at the store that's near the church so they can get a cup.

"Is it okay to take coffee in church?" he asks.

Trinity giggles. "You are so cute. Yes, it's okay."

They pull into the small lot of the country store that's on the way. Hand in hand they walk in and go down the aisle where the assortment of junk food and drinks are plentiful. Since they had to skip breakfast both of them are hungry, but eating will have to wait until later. Gates mentions possibly getting some lunch as soon as they get out of church.

***

Derrick

Neither of them see Derrick as they turn the end of the aisle and walk to the coffee bar, talking as they go. The unmistakable sound of her voice catches Derrick by surprise and he turns toward her in complete shock. There she stands, only a few feet away, unaware of his presence.

His first emotion is anger, then he sees how beautiful she is. When he realizes she's with the man next to her, the anger returns ten-fold and he has no choice but to confront them. Not that he would have waited anyhow.

"Trinity," he says her name with a shaky voice. At first, he doesn't think she hears him so he repeats her name louder. "Trinity!"

The sound of her name fills the air and immediately she recognizes the voice. It's one she'll never be able to get out of her head. Fear envelopes her and she stops stirring her coffee. She freezes and doesn't want to turn around, but Gates does. By her reaction and because another man speaks her name with a tone of anger, he knows who it is. He turns toward Derrick with every nerve, every cell in his body ready for action. His instincts kick in and as Trinity slowly turns toward the man she fears most, one of Gates' hands rests on her waist as the other prepares to reach behind his back.

With a quivering voice, full of emotion and fear, Trinity asks, "Derrick…why are you here? Why can't you leave me alone?"

"I want you to come home with me, honey. Let's not make a scene. I don't want any trouble. I only want to take you home where you belong. Please, Trinity. Let's go home."

"She doesn't want to be with you," Gates interrupts. "She is afraid of you. Can't you see that?"

Their eyes meet; Derrick isn't able to control himself and his words burst forth with enough intensity to turn every head in the building. "Who are you? She belongs to me!" Derrick throws his cup to the floor and coffee splatters over everything around it. He pulls his 9mm from his jacket and points it at them. "She is coming with me and she's coming now! I am not playing games!"

Screams fill the store once everyone sees what is happening. The store clerk pushes the red button beneath the counter, alerting the police department, and ducks down onto the floor. Gates wants to reach for his gun, but he knows he won't be able to get it before Derrick gets a shot off. He can't take the chance of Trinity getting shot.

"Derrick, please don't do this," she begs him as tears burn her eyes.

"Like I said, you are coming home with me. I will change sweetheart, just give me a chance," he tells her as he continues to point the gun at them. "What can he do for you that I can't? I love you. Please don't make me do this. Come home."

"Derrick…" His name leaves her lips, a pained whisper, and she takes a step forward. As she moves, Derrick begins to lower his gun. In an instant Gates is pulling his out from behind his back. Derrick sees the movement; he's close enough to grab Trinity before Gates is fully prepared. Fear courses through Trinity like a lightning strike. Her eyes bulge; she can see Gates wants to do something, anything, to keep her safe.

"Don't…even…think about it!" Derrick screams at him, barely loud enough to be heard over Trinity's frightening shriek. She struggles in his iron grip, caught between two men who are both willing to kill over her. With her fingers digging into Derrick's arm, she cries out, begging for him to let her go and he begins to back away.

***

Trinity

"She's mine! Back off now or I will shoot!" he threatens. Gates takes a step forward as Derrick backs away with no intention of giving in. It is obvious to all that Derrick is willing to die for her. In her head, Trinity pleads with God to help them, to save them from this disaster.

Another voice rings through the air, one no one expected to hear.

"Drop the guns and put your hands above your heads!" a deputy yells at them. A moment later the police officer walks around where Trinity can see him.

Three men.

Three guns.

All of them cocked and ready to fire.

Trinity doesn't think. Her instincts kick in and she bites down as hard as she can on Derrick's arm, drawing blood and causing him to scream. It breaks his focus on Gates and the police officer. Immediately, Gates begins to charge even though the police officer is right there. Derrick loses what little rational thinking he has and pulls the trigger. The piercing sound that rings through the air almost shatters her eardrums, but not before she sees the impact of the bullet hitting Gates, knocking him to the ground. Screaming Gates' name, she kicks Derrick in the groin, causing him to double over and loosen his hold on her enough to break free. He turns the gun on her as she runs.

With tear-filled eyes, she is barely able to see where she's going and doesn't know if she will be shot as well. When she hears the next shot she falls, unsure if it is meant for her. Another shot rings through the air, then silence. With her face down she trembles in fear, but doesn't feel any physical pain. Raising up, she looks behind her and sees Derrick lying on the floor, motionless, and the officer running to her.

"Ma'am, are you okay?" he asks when he gets to her. "Are you okay?"

Trinity is speechless and feels like throwing up. Sirens fill the air and she hears them pull into the parking lot. All she can think about is Gates. Is he alive or dead? She scrambles to him, afraid it is too late.

"Gates!" she screams as she falls to the floor next to him. His eyes are barely open but he looks at her. "Please don't die! Please, don't leave me!"

"I love you, Trinity," he whispers, reaching to touch her face when the paramedics rush in and push her to the side. She scrambles alongside not wanting to leave him, refusing to be left behind as they put him in the back of the ambulance. She begs the paramedics to let her go with them, crying and lying about being his wife. She isn't thinking clearly; she only knows she wants to be with him.

As the ambulance drives away with the siren blaring, the man who brought hell into her life lies dead, surrounded by cops and the coroner. The man who brings her love is lying beside her, fighting for his life, urgently on the way to the hospital.

"God, please I beg You, please don't take him from me! Please, God, I love him and need him!" she prays, not caring who hears or what they think.

She watches the paramedic do his job, and she feels like her world is falling apart right in front of her.

***

Once they arrive at the hospital, Trinity has no choice but to sit in the emergency room waiting area, alone. She is not allowed in the operating room. She sits with her face buried in her hands, hoping, praying…and afraid.

"Trinity!"

Lifting her tear-streaked face, Trinity sees Gloria rushing to her side. She called Gloria when she had nobody else to call. She doesn't want to wait alone as Gates is in surgery. Gloria hugs her. "How are you doing?"

"I'm terrified," Trinity answers. "The cops just left after asking me questions about what happened, and I thought I was going to have a nervous breakdown. I don't care about their stupid questions. I just want to see Gates!" She breaks into tears again and leans into the arms of her friend, letting everything out. Gloria holds and comforts her, allowing her to cry as long as she needs to. After a few minutes Trinity lifts her head and pulls herself together. Gloria begins talking.

"I can only imagine what you must be feeling sweetie, so let's do this. Don't worry about the cops right now and do your best to not worry about Gates. He's in good hands with the doctors and more importantly, he's in God's hands. Do you feel like praying? Let's ask God to take care of him and have faith that He will."

"Yes, please."

Gloria takes Trinity's hands in hers and begins. "God, our Lord and Savior, You already know what has transpired today, and You already know the heartache that is felt. In the other room is a great man, a hero to this child of Yours sitting with me. You and only You can do what is needed to be done and only You have the power to make him whole again. We ask You to place Your loving hands upon Gates as he is in surgery and to heal him. We ask You, if it's Your will, to make the doctors and nurses work Your miracle on him, and we ask that You give Trinity the strength, courage, acceptance, and faith it takes to get through this with him. In Your holy name we pray, amen."

"Amen," Trinity murmurs and squeezes Gloria's hand. "Thank you."

"You're welcome. How long has he been in surgery?"

"About two hours. I have no idea how long it'll be."

"He's going to be okay. You have to have faith. I'm here with you until you know something."

"Thank you, that really means a lot."

Together they sit and wait, watching the clock. As time ticks by slowly they grow more concerned, but Gloria tries to break the monotony.

"Have you eaten anything? Do you want some coffee or something?" Gloria asks her.

Trinity shakes her head. "No, we overslept and didn't have time for breakfast. I don't think I can eat anything right now, but a cup of coffee would be great."

"Stay here, I'll be right back. I could use a cup myself. Do you like anything in it?"

"Cream and two sugars, please, and thank you."

"You're welcome," Gloria says as she leaves to find the cafeteria.

Trinity sits back and closes her eyes as her friend walks down the hall, and says her own personal prayer for probably the fifth time.

"I know I'm not the best child You have and I know I have my struggles Lord, but I beg You to please get Gates through this. I don't think You would have put us in each other's lives for nothing then take him away. I believe in You and love You with all that I am. I have fallen in love with Gates. I haven't told him yet, but it's true. I need him with me. Lord. Please, keep him here with me. In Your name I pray, amen."

Sitting in the waiting room, along with a crowd that seems to be growing, she tries not to think about what the day has held for her so far, but there is no possible way of escaping it. All they wanted to do was go to church, but something else, something evil had other plans. Her ex-boyfriend did exactly what Gates said he would do. He came after her and now because of her, Gates is in surgery fighting for his life. She feels guilty. Tears threaten to escape again, but she fights them back.

"Have faith, girl! Have faith! You have to keep it together," she tells herself.

She watches a couple walk in with their child and Trinity smiles weakly at them. The little girl looks like she's about four years old, with blonde hair down to her shoulders and beautiful blue eyes.

She looks at Trinity, smiles, and asks what her name is.

"My name is Trinity; what is yours?" she responds, trying to be friendly.

"Hope. My name is Hope."

Trinity feels a twinge in her heart as if God is telling her something. She feels a miracle taking place right in front of her.

"That's a beautiful name," she tells the little girl as her parents sit and watch their daughter strike up a conversation with a complete stranger as if it's the most natural thing in the world.

"Thank you. I like your name a lot, too. I'm here because my brother is getting his tonsils out. Why are you here?"

Trinity isn't sure exactly what to say, so she simply says, "Someone I love very much is hurt and he's having surgery."

Hope's eyes suddenly seem to glow. It catches Trinity off guard when she feels the child's tiny hand cover her own.

"Your friend is okay now. You can stop being afraid."

Trinity feels her heart lighten with the child's words, and can't stop feeling as if she is witnessing a true miracle. The little girl smiles at her and releases her hand. Her parents call her, saying they need to go. Hope hugs Trinity, making her want to cry. She watches Hope and her family leave the room mere seconds before Gloria walks back in. Gloria sees the expression on Trinity's face and asks if she's okay.

As Trinity takes her coffee she asks, "Did you

see that couple and little girl who walked around the corner as you came in?"

Gloria shakes her head. "I didn't see anyone."

"Are you sure? You should have walked right past them. They literally walked around the corner only seconds before you did."

"No, sorry, I didn't see anyone. Why?"

Trinity feels it. She believes it. She suddenly feels the presence of God and she knows, just like Hope said to her, that Gates is okay and she doesn't have to be afraid anymore. She tells Gloria what happened while she was gone and how it affects her.

"Sounds like God is definitely here with us, dear. I wish I could have witnessed that, but I have a feeling it was meant for only you."

Trinity wipes away a tear and nods. "I think so, too."

A doctor begins to walk toward them, and by the look on his face, Trinity can tell things went well. A feeling of gratitude fills her as he tells them they were able to get the bullet out. It wasn't as bad as they first thought, although it did barely miss his heart. He says the bullet entered Gates' left shoulder right above and to the left of his heart. He's a lucky man and should have a relatively easy recovery, but they will be keeping him for at least a few days. Trinity hugs the doctor and thanks him.

"When can I see him?"

"I'll tell the nurse to come get you once they have him in a room and more comfortable. It shouldn't be long, but most likely he will be unconscious. I gave him something strong for the pain."

Trinity thanks him again as he turns and walks away; she's shocked she doesn't burst into tears. She sits beside Gloria and tries to be patient as they talk about what happened. Gloria sits and listens as Trinity tells her the truth. She tells Gloria some of her history with Derrick and the real reason why she moved to Moneta. She opens up to Gloria more. It isn't long before a nurse comes to get them to show them to Gates' room. They follow the nurse and when they get there, Gloria says she will stay if Trinity needs her, otherwise she's going to leave her with Gates so they can have their privacy.

"Thank you for everything. You are a true friend," Trinity tells her and hugs her goodbye.

"Call me if you need anything."

She watches her friend leave, then takes a deep breath as she walks into Gates' room. When she sees him lying on the bed with tubes sticking out of him and his shoulder wrapped up like an Eskimo, her emotions come close to taking control again. She's thankful that he's asleep so he can't see her this way. She sits in the chair beside his bed and watches him. Her heart goes out to him and her hand trembles when she reaches out to tenderly touch his. She doesn't want to wake him, but only to feel her skin against his.

Part of her wants to make sure she isn't imagining things, to see if he is really there with her and alive. When her fingers touch his arm her lips tremble and she is no longer able to hold back the tears. They flow freely down her face as she thanks God for keeping him alive. She lowers her face and cries silently in her hands.

Once she has control of her emotions, Trinity sits up and decides she won't leave until she is able to speak to Gates. There is no way she can leave knowing he will want to see her when he opens his eyes. It doesn't matter how long it takes; she isn't moving.

An hour passes and her eyes grow heavy and she falls asleep in the chair. It feels like only a short time passes; she isn't sure if she's dreaming or not, but she hears Gates saying her name. She opens her eyes and bolts upright when she notices he is looking at her.

"Oh, Gates!" she cries and stands over him. "How are you feeling, baby?"

"I'm in a lot of pain, but seeing you here makes everything better," he croaks, obviously with a parched throat.

"I'll get a nurse," she tells him and immediately walks into the hall looking for someone to help. "I need a nurse, please. He's awake and is in pain."

Trinity walks back into the room with two nurses hustling behind her. She stands back and watches as they check his vitals, ask him some questions, and one of them says she will bring him something for pain right away. As she watches the nurses take care of him, she is still stunned by the day's events and feels numb all over. When the nurses leave, he looks at her, motioning with his finger for her to come to him. She takes his hand in hers and leans down, kisses him tenderly and a tear falls on his face before either can catch it. She wipes it away, telling him she's sorry, which makes him smile.

"Please, don't."

"Don't what? Am I hurting you?" she asks and stands back up.

"Don't make me laugh. It hurts to laugh."

"Oh, okay. I didn't know I did anything funny."

He looks at her, squeezes her hand, and says, "Trinity…I love you." Her heart melts and she honestly knows she can say the same thing.

"I love you, too."

Time stands still as she touches his lips with hers, trying to be careful to not touch him anywhere else for fear of causing him pain. At the same time both of their hearts intertwine, unseen, but certainly felt as the kiss bonds their love for each other.

Chapter Fourteen

It's eleven o'clock; Trinity has been at the hospital the entire day, with no intention of leaving Gates alone. She has already flipped through the stations on the small television that hangs from the corner, and hasn't found a single thing worth watching. She truly hates the remote. For some insane reason, they made the channel selector where it can only go forward, so if she is searching for something to watch, she has to go through all of the stations several times before she finds anything, if she is lucky. Gates softly snores as he sleeps from the pain medicine, so she mainly sits and watches him. He looks like he's having a dream and she wonders what it's about. She hopes it's about her and she smiles.

With nothing more to do than twiddle her thumbs, she thinks about what happened earlier. Thoughts of the events that so rapidly took place, and Gates he almost died for her, make her chest hurt and her throat feel like a frog is stuck in the middle of it. Stinging tears fill her eyes as she thinks about how her life would be if that nightmare had happened. If she had lost him because of her. Part of her blames herself, although she knows she shouldn't. She had no control over Derrick or what he did. But, seeing Gates lying here in a hospital bed, blessed to be alive, she can't help it. She wouldn't be able to cope if he had been killed.

Even though she no longer has any love in her for Derrick, she still can't help but feel sadness not only for him dying, but for his loved ones as well. She closes her eyes and says a silent prayer for his family.

Her cell phone begins vibrating on the table beside her and she quickly grabs it so it won't wake Gates. Her legs and back ache from sitting for so long, and when she stands to walk out of the room, she feels ten years older than usual. When she gets in the hall she answers, having already seen that it's Katherine.

"Hey, how is he? How are you?" Katherine asks her right away.

"He's better than I thought he would be. I was terrified when it happened and before the doctor talked to me, but he's going to be okay."

"I can only imagine what you were feeling. How are you, sweetheart? I know you have to be torn up inside. I certainly would be. I would have called earlier, but I didn't have the television on so I didn't see the news until a few minutes ago. I'm terribly sorry. Do you need anything? I'm coming to see him tomorrow when visiting hours are open again. I know they won't let me see him right now."

Trinity surprisingly laughs and comments, "I could use a shower, a change of clothes, something decent to eat, you name it, and I know he would love to see you."

"You poor thing; I know you have to be exhausted."

"I'm tired, but I can't leave him. He almost died because of me."

When those words fall from her lips, Trinity can't hold back the bout of emotions she has been fighting. The sharp intake of breath is heard on the other end of the line.

"Sweetie, don't be so hard on yourself. I know he loves you and he would do anything in this world for you. I saw how he looked at you when you were here."

"I love him, too," Trinity manages to whisper. "I am so madly in love with him; that's another reason this is so hard."

"Have you been praying? Do you have a Bible there with you?"

"Oh yeah, trust me, I've been praying…a lot. Thank you for asking about a Bible. I didn't even think about looking, but I bet there's one in the nightstand beside his bed. I'll look when I get off the phone."

"You go ahead then and I will see you both tomorrow. I'll be praying for you tonight."

"I really appreciate that and thank you for calling. I'll tell him you called."

Trinity walks quietly back into the dimly lit room to find him still sleeping. She leans against the wall for a moment and lets her eyes rest on his face.

With only minimal lighting, the shadows and stubble on his face cause him to appear more scruffy than normal. Her heart flutters as she stares at him. Her breathing is slightly ragged as she continues to battle her emotions, but she isn't going to give in.

After a couple of minutes she opens the drawer in the nightstand as quietly as she can, and is thrilled to see a Holy Bible sitting there, waiting for her. She specifically wants to look up a passage on faith; if her memory is accurate she will find it in the book of Matthew. Before she looks for it, though, she kneels beside the chair and talks to her Lord and Savior.

"Jesus, You know all and You already know what needs to be done, but I ask You to bless my heart and soul as I look for the right passage to read not only for myself, but for Gates as well. I also want to ask You, Lord Jesus, to please lay Your loving hands upon him and heal him from his pain, and to guide us together, if it's Your will, along whatever journey You have planned out for us. In Your name I pray, amen."

Sitting in the chair, she looks in Matthew and easily finds the passage she wants.

Matthew 14:30-31: But when he saw the wind, he was afraid; and beginning to sink, he cried out, saying, Lord, save me. And immediately Jesus stretched forth his hand, and took hold of him, and saith unto him, O thou of little faith, wherefore didst thou doubt?

Trinity's heart beams from reading the Lord's Word. To her, Jesus is telling her that no matter what storms she has to face He will always be there as long as she has faith. She remembers another passage that has deep meaning and turns to it.

Matthew 17:20: And he saith unto them, Because of your little faith: for verily I say unto you, If ye have faith as a grain of mustard seed, ye shall say unto this mountain, Remove hence to yonder place; and it shall remove; and nothing shall be impossible unto you.

She continues to read more, wanting and needing as much of God's Word and strength as she can get. She finds a verse on strength.

Isaiah 40:31: but they that wait for Jehovah shall renew their strength; they shall mount up with wings as eagles; they shall run, and not be weary; they shall walk and not faint.

After reading for a while longer her emotions are under control and she feels tremendously better. She closes the Bible and her eyes, and says "Thank You" to Jesus for blessing her with His words. When she opens her eyes, she smiles at Gates because she knows everything will be okay. He will be okay. They, as a couple, will be okay.

***

About three o'clock in the morning, Trinity

wakes from pain in her back from sitting in the chair for so long. Moaning softly, as she stretches and rubs the base of her back, she sees Gates is awake and watching her. He smiles and she all but forgets her discomfort. She immediately stands next to him, taking his hand in hers. Her heart feels like it is bursting within her chest.

"I can't believe you are still here. Have you been here all day?" he asks.

"Are you okay? How are you feeling?" she replies without answering his question.

Smiling at her he answers, "I'm in some pain, but I will get through it, and you didn't answer me."

Pressing her lips together, she nods and answers, "Yes, I've been here all day. I can't leave you. Do you want me to get a nurse?"

"Will you, please?"

Leaning down she kisses him lightly and says, "Yes, I will, and I love you."

"I love you too, and thank you."

It's early in the morning so when she gets to the door, Trinity looks both ways for a nurse. The hall is empty, but she can hear people talking so she quickly goes toward the voices. When she sees a few nurses and a doctor behind the nurses' desk, she gets their attention.

"Can someone bring my boyfriend something for his pain? He's awake and hurting."

"I'll be there in a moment to check on him," says the doctor.

"Thank you."

Trinity turns to walk back to Gates' room, and realizes—for the first time she said out loud that he is her boyfriend. The idea makes her feel warm inside and she loves how the words make her feel, but is he? She knows they are definitely more than friends; they have already confessed their love but haven't actually made it official. Then again, when have they had a chance with all the insanity that's happened? She wants to talk about it, but knows it can wait until later. When she walks back into his room she can see he has been trying to sit up with obvious difficulty.

"Here, let me help you!" she says and hurries to his side.

"Thanks," he grunts in response.

"The doctor is on his way to talk to you and will probably give you something for the pain."

He blows out a heavy breath and winces from the slight movement. "It's going to be a real joy healing from this. It's been a while since I have had the pleasure."

"What? You've been shot before?" she asks, obvious shock in her voice.

"Unfortunately, yes. Twice, during the time I was in the Marines. Getting shot again is certainly a reminder that it wasn't fun then, either."

"What happened?"

"I'll tell you about it in a few minutes, once I get something for the pain."

"You poor baby," she coos and caresses his arm. She leans in and kisses him on his cheek.

"I have to tell you I'm pretty sure I could get used to all of this special treatment from you."

"Oh, trust me, there's a lot more where that came from."

"Okay, sorry it took so long," the doctor interrupts as he barges in. "My attention was suddenly required by several patients at once. Good to see you are awake. So, tell me, on a scale from one to ten, how much pain are you in?"

"Since we are playing a game, I will give it a ten," Gates answers, with a look that questions the doctor's sanity.

The doctor listens to his heartbeat and checks his pulse. As he checks Gates' wound to see if it's bleeding, he says, "Sorry, I didn't mean to sound insensitive. I have no doubt you need something; I only need to know so I can tell the nurse what to give you and how much. I'll let her know now."

Gates thanks the doctor as he leaves and shakes his head. Trinity looks at him and blows him a kiss.

"Is there anything else you need? Do you want me to get you something to drink or eat?"

"I'm starved to be honest, but I'll ask the nurse to get me something when she gets here. Maybe she'll be able to scrounge up a sandwich or something. As late as it is, you wouldn't be able to get anything since I'm sure everything is closed. Aren't you hungry?"

"Actually, I could eat right now, too. If I had a car I could go and get us something."

"Oh, that reminds me! What happened to my Jeep? Is it still at the store or did it get impounded?"

"I called the store manager earlier and asked if it could stay there until I can get it tomorrow. I hope you don't mind. I will have Gloria take me and I'll drive it back here."

"Of course, that's fine. I totally forgot all about it

being there. Yes, please do go and get it, thank you."

"While I'm at it, I'll run by the house and check on Sheeba, grab a few things for us both, and bring us back something decent to eat."

"All of that sounds great, but what I would rather you do before you come back is get some sleep in your bed, or at least a long nap. I know you have to be exhausted."

Frowning, she has to agree she is feeling tired from the lack of sleep and her back hurts from sitting in the chair for hours, not to mention the stress of all the events that have taken place.

"That's probably not a bad idea. My bed would feel great, but will you be okay while I'm gone? I'll feel guilty about leaving you."

He grins and tells her, "You seem to forget that I am a big boy and I'm in good hands. You get some rest and when you wake up, take a shower, put on some clean clothes, play with Sheeba, and whatever else you need to do, then come back to see me. I'll be fine, I promise."

She can't help but giggle and agrees. "Okay, I'll try to get some rest. I'm sure Sheeba misses you. It's too bad I can't bring her."

"She doesn't miss me. Well, maybe a little, but I'm sure she misses her momma more. I bought her thinking she would be my dog, but boy did I get that wrong. It's a good thing I love you."

Leaning down until their noses touch, Trinity says "I love you, too."

After a small kiss, the nurse finally walks in with some pain medicine and water, grinning at them.

They ask her if they can get something to eat and surprisingly, she says there may be a couple of sandwiches in the refrigerator. While they are waiting, Trinity's phone begins to ring and she retrieves it from her purse. When she looks at it, she tells Gates who it is, which makes him smile.

"Hey, girl are you okay?" Trinity asks her. "You are up terribly late."

"I can't sleep from worrying about Gates. Is he okay? Are you okay?"

"Oh, I'm sorry, and yes we are both good. Well, better, I should say. Would you like to talk to him? He's awake."

Katherine was suddenly happier when Trinity handed Gates the phone. They talk for a few minutes and she hears him tell her what room he's in and that it isn't too late for her to visit quickly. He tells Katherine as he watches Trinity's expression that she needs to get the Jeep and some sleep. She eyes him suspiciously and gives him a stern look. When he ends the call without giving Trinity a chance to talk to Katherine again, she wants to know what that was all about.

"She'll be here in about an hour to get you," he tells her with a mischievous grin.

"What? It's so early...or late, whatever. I can wait until I can get a hold of Gloria. She doesn't have to do that now. Besides, they won't let her visit you now. Not at this hour."

He grimaces when he moves slightly, then says, "Too late. She said she was wide awake and even though visiting hours aren't open, she said she would pop her head in long enough to say 'Hi' and get you. You need some rest, Trinity. Please, don't be mad."

"I'm not mad. I'm caught off guard a little, but not mad. Besides, you need your rest too. I'll go and get the Jeep, do what I need to do, and be back probably in the afternoon, if not earlier."

"Sounds good."

The nurse walks in with two sandwiches and a couple of small ginger ales. They thank her and devour the food within minutes. They watch television as they wait for Katherine and the time flies by.

They hear her in the hall telling someone she's picking Trinity up, and only wants to say hello to Gates. Surprisingly, they allow her to. With a huge grin she greets Gates, but is extremely careful about not hurting him when she lightly hugs him and kisses his cheek.

"You have no idea how worried I have been! I have been praying my tail off!" she tells him.

"Thank you, I really appreciate that and thank you for coming to take her home. She is stubborn."

"You're welcome. I wish I could stay, but I'm lucky they let me in at all."

"I'm not stubborn," Trinity protests with a fake expression of hurt.

"Okay, if you say so," he replies, rolling his eyes.

"Well, stubborn or not I guess we should go before they say something. Are you ready?"

"I guess," Trinity says, and leans down to kiss Gates goodbye. "I'll be back as soon as I can."

"Okay, but get some sleep first, and be careful."

"Okay, okay…I love you."

"I love you, too."

Trinity and Katherine walk out of the room and even though she knows Gates is right about her need to go home for a while, guilt from leaving him still consumes her. She and Katherine have a long talk on the way home. They are able to tell each other more openly about themselves and within a short amount of time create a sister-like bond. When they get to the store where the Jeep was left, Katherine follows her to the house to make sure she's okay. Trinity talks her into staying the night so she won't have to drive back so late. They stay up another hour and play with Sheeba, who's ecstatic about her momma being home and bringing a new human to play with. Once they are talked out, Katherine sleeps on the sofa, and Trinity falls asleep almost instantly when her head touches the pillow.

Visions of walking through a park filled with glamour and sunshine fill her dreams. The trees are full of leaves; the flowers are alive and glowing with their beauty. She can see herself alone, but smiling as she walks past a bench with full, green bushes on either side and the sound of Sheeba's barking in the air. In her dream, she laughs and kneels down to love on her beautiful dog and Gates walks into view, grinning from ear to ear. As he gets closer her heart melts with the pure joy and love she has for him. The dream doesn't last nearly as long as she would like, but the last thing she sees before it disappears is them kissing and their lips moving, whispering their love for each other.

Chapter Fifteen

Later that morning, Trinity is awakened by a tremendous pounding in her temples. When the light touches her eyes, she groans loudly and quickly shuts them again. She is still tired from being up for so long yesterday, but knows she needs to get out of bed. With the way she feels, moving is one of the last things she wants to do. She peeks through her barely opened eyelids at the clock and sees it's after ten. She slept a little longer than she intended, but would still love to sleep some more. Instead, she slowly slides out from beneath the sheets and realizes Sheeba isn't with her. She remembers Katherine stayed over and slept on the sofa. Is she still here? She shuffles out into the hall and can hear her talking to the dog like she's human. It warms Trinity's heart.

"Good morning," she moans when she walks in the room. With one hand, she tries to hide her eyes from the bright sunlight beaming through the open blinds. Immediately, Sheeba is jumping for joy to see her. "Good morning to you too, baby."

"Good morning; how did you sleep? I was going to wake you about noon if you hadn't got up. You needed your sleep," Katherine says.

"I slept great, but I have an awful headache. Can you do me a huge favor while I look for some ibuprofen?"

Already knowing what the request is going to be, Katherine answers. "I've already taken her out, about an hour ago after I made some coffee."

"Thank you so much. I'll be right back." Trinity steps into the bathroom in search of something to kill her pain before it immobilizes her. After finding what she wants and swallowing three pills, she walks back into the living room and eases herself onto the couch next to her friend. "So, what are your plans for the day? I actually need to get back to the house and get started on a couple of things, but I was hoping to go with you to see Gates first. I'll follow you so I can go home from there."

"Once this headache is better I'm going to take a shower then get some things together for Gates and me. Then I'm going to go somewhere and get him something good to eat. Well, for both of us actually, so if you are going with me you can eat with us if you like."

"Sounds like a plan to me."

Trinity sits with her eyes closed and can feel Sheeba between her legs wanting her attention, but she doesn't feel up to it at the moment. Katherine suspects something other than her head is bothering her.

"Do you want to talk about it?" Katherine asks

her.

"About what?"

"Whatever is bothering you."

Trinity is caught off guard by her friend's observation. She hasn't said anything and has been denying it herself, but what happened to Derrick is certainly in the back of her mind. Maybe, she thinks, she pushed it away and that is the cause of her head hurting. Even though he was the cause of so much pain and heartache in her life, she didn't want to see him killed. She only wanted to be left alone, allowed to move forward in her life in search of happiness. She has to admit…it is painful.

Her head starts to throb worse as tears threaten to overwhelm her again. She isn't ready to deal with this right now. She has other things to be concerned about, but her thoughts aren't cooperating with her emotions and she breaks down into a fit of sobs. Katherine slides closer and pulls her into her arms. She allows Trinity to get it out without any interruption. A few minutes later, once she catches her breath, Trinity apologizes.

"You have no reason to be sorry. You've had a tremendous amount of stress in your life for quite some time, especially over the past twenty-four hours. It's natural to be a blubbering mess. I have no doubt I would be."

Sniffling and wiping her eyes, Trinity replies, "You're right, but I was trying my best to be strong."

"For who, Gates?"

Trinity nods. "He needs me right now."

Katherine smiles and assures her. "What he

needs most from you right now is for you to be yourself. If that means not always being strong, then so be it. Knowing him the way I do, I'm sure he would rather see you cry and let things out than to be stressing yourself. He loves you. You have nothing to worry about with him."

Trinity smiles. "That means a lot, I appreciate it."

She talks to Katherine about Derrick, how it hurt her to see him die, and how she wishes things could have been different for him. She says she didn't wish anything more for the two of them, but that he would have been able to move on without her and bettered himself in some way. She says she doesn't wish what happened to him on anyone. More tears flow and shake her petite form, but when they stop she feels better. Even her headache eases enough to start getting ready.

"I'm going to call Gates real quick and see how he's doing, then I'll get ready so we can go. Thank you again for being here for me."

"You are very welcome. That's what friends do, right?"

"Right."

Katherine watches television while Trinity walks into her bedroom to do what she has to do. Surprisingly, the dog stays with Katherine. Gates is doing fine, but he sounds like they have some powerful pain killers in him. At least he isn't hurting. Trinity tells him they will be there in a couple of hours when she finishes getting ready.

"Can you bring me something to eat, please?" he mumbles in his drugged state. "I can't take too

173

much more of this lousy hospital food."

"Of course honey; what would you like? I can get you something from Subtrak, or a burger from somewhere…"

"Surprise me. I don't care what it is."

She laughs. "Okay, I'll get you something good that I know you'll like.

"I love you, Trinity." He sounds like he's falling asleep, but she knows he means what he says. "I thank God for you."

"I love you, too, Gates, and I'm very, very thankful for you, too. You don't know how much."

"I don't mean to be rude, honey, but I can barely keep my eyes open from this pain medicine. I will see you when you get here."

Her heart goes out to him. "I'll be there soon."

Trinity sits on the edge of her bed with her face in the palms of her hands. She wishes more than anything that she could take away what happened, but she knows she can't. All she can do is pray and have faith.

"God, You already know what needs to be done, but I have to ask that You help Gates. Please, lay Your loving hands on him and heal him. Please take away his pain. I also want to ask You, Lord, to comfort the family of Derrick and his friends when they have to go through their pain of losing him. I pray that they will be able to deal with their loss. In Your name I pray, amen."

For the moment finished talking to the One she knows will always be with her, Trinity quickly takes her shower and gets things together for them both. She hopes the hospital will allow her to stay the night with Gates.

***

An hour and a half later Trinity and Katherine walk into Gates' room. He's still knocked out from whatever the doctors gave him. They quietly sit the duffle bag Trinity packed for him on the floor and the dinner plate on the table by the bed. She hopes he will like what she chose for him to eat.

Katherine motions for Trinity to follow her into the hall.

"I really want to see him, but he looks like he's really out of it. I have some things I need to do so I'm going to go ahead and head home. Please, tell him I was here and that I'm sorry I couldn't stay, but I will call later to talk to him."

"Okay, I will. I know he'll understand, as do I. Thank you again for everything."

They hug goodbye. Trinity walks back in the room and sits next to the bed. The aroma of the food she brought wafts through the air, and she hopes the nurses will reheat it for him when he wakes up. She sees his shoulder wrapped in what looks like an incredible amount of gauze and again has to fight back tears. She refuses to have him open his eyes and see her crying. Besides, she talked to God and knows everything will be okay. She can see his eyelids twitching and wonders what he's dreaming about. A moment later he sighs and moves his head. When he opens his eyes she immediately smiles for him. His gaze rests on her and he sleepily grins.

"Hey beautiful," he murmurs.

She takes his hand in hers and replies, "Hey to you, too, handsome. How are you feeling? Did you sleep okay?"

"I'm okay. They have me on some drugs so my shoulder doesn't hurt as much. I guess I slept okay. I was dreaming about someone very special to me," he slurs.

"And who might that be?" she asks, knowing it was her but going along with the joke. "Were you dreaming about Sheeba?"

He laughs, but has to restrain himself so he doesn't hurt his shoulder. "Very funny, but no it wasn't her. I was dreaming about you."

"I was hoping it was me. What was I doing in your dream?"

It's his turn to play with her and he declines the chance to reveal his dream. "I can't tell you. It's a surprise for later."

"You can't tell me?" She feigns hurt. "How long do I have to wait?"

"That depends on you," he tells her with a mischievous grin.

"Okay, so now a riddle too. Okay, I will just take this yummy plate of food and give it to one of the nurses, then," she says with a wink.

"You wouldn't."

She laughs and places it back on the table. "Of course I wouldn't. I hope you like it."

"What is it? It smells great."

"I stopped at an Italian place down the street and got some lasagna. I got enough for both of us, but I was waiting for you."

Trinity does something she has never done for a

man before. She feeds him. They are laughing at each other and enjoying the lasagna when the doctor walks in.

He is pleased with Gates' spirits. "I want to watch you to make sure you don't get an infection. Assuming all goes well, you'll be able to go home in a couple of days."

"I'm ready to go now."

"No, I don't think so. It's better to be safe than sorry."

After they finish eating, Trinity wants to talk about what's next, now that she doesn't "need" protection. She isn't a hundred percent sure what Gates wants, and honestly, she isn't too sure what she wants. She knows she has fallen in love with him, but living in his house with their deepening feelings can easily become difficult.

"So, I was wondering if we can have a talk about something, if you feel up to it."

"Sure, I think I can handle a conversation with you," he jokes.

She grins at his attempt to make her laugh. "Now that things are different...I mean now that I don't have to worry anymore about being in danger from Derrick, what is going to happen now?"

His smile turns into a more serious expression. He thinks about his answer before replying. "I assume you are talking about us and where we go from here."

"Yeah, that's what I want to talk about."

"Are you unsure about how you feel?"

"About you? No, I'm definitely sure about my feelings for you." She pauses and takes a deep breath. "It's just that, well I have to be honest and I think you will agree, that we both have desires that are difficult to keep under control. As much as I would like to allow these feelings to happen, I don't feel comfortable about it because I don't want to feel guilty afterward."

"Because of your faith?"

"Yes." She pauses. "Please understand."

"I do…" he says, but she thinks she can see hurt in his eyes. "So I guess we need to figure something out. I will never do anything to make you uncomfortable."

"I know and I don't want to make you uncomfortable either. I have an idea, though, that I think we can both live with."

"I'm all ears."

"I haven't talked to her about it yet, but I was thinking about asking Gloria, since she lives alone, if she would be interested in a roommate. I will get a job, of course, and rent from her. She lives in Moneta so we can still see each other, and it wouldn't be putting pressure on either of us."

He presses his lips together, giving him a serious expression. With a gaze filled with compassion and love he nods. "I'm willing to do whatever you think is best. I have to admit that over a short period of time we have fallen into a relationship we weren't expecting. I think it's a great idea, to be honest."

Surprised that the talk she dreaded is going so well, she asks, "Really? You think it's a good thing then?"

"Yes, I really do. If you think about it, it will give us the space we need, such as you being able to not worry about how you dress with me in the house, or when either one of us is coming out of the bathroom, you know, things like that. And we can take time to really get to know each other the way we should."

Her face beams with delight that he understands. "Thank you. You have no idea how much it means to me that you are willing to do this. I was actually a little worried that you wouldn't understand."

"That's what I'm talking about," he says to her and holds her hand. "In time, we will learn how the other thinks, how we both feel about certain things, and when we do spend time together it will always be great. Don't get me wrong...in the past few weeks I have grown used to you being with me, so I will miss you. It'll take some getting used to again, being alone."

"I'll miss you, too."

"When do you think you'll talk to Gloria?"

"I'll wait until Sunday when I see her at church and I guess I will stay at your place until you heal a little more so I can take care of you."

"You are going to spoil me."

"Don't get too used to it," she teases.

Chapter Sixteen

Gates

The last couple of days at the hospital go by slower for Gates than he wants, but Trinity being with him most of the time makes the wait more tolerable. When she isn't there he has time to think about a lot of things. More things than he wants to have bombarding his mind at the same time. He's been out of the service for years, and hasn't been shot at or come close to dying until now. The experience made his eyes open more than they used to be. Certainly, with living on the lake, nature, and his lifestyle of being more down to earth he isn't the man he used to be, but he begins to think about his spiritual life…and how Trinity fits into all of that.

One thing he is quickly loving about her, among a lot of other things, is her passion to live how she believes to be the right way to live. She loves going to church, reading the Bible, praying, and when he hears her say she wants to live for Jesus Christ, he wonders how that makes her feel. He has never given his life to Christ before.

Is his brush with death a hint from God? Is he being given a chance to get himself together with God? He needs to seriously think about making some changes in his life. He bought them both a Bible; so since he has one, he should probably start reading it and continue going to church with her. Not only because she's going, but because he needs the lessons being taught there. He doesn't tell her because he doesn't want her to worry any more than he knows she already is, but the fact that he could've died did shake him up. Honestly…it scared him. Enough to where he can feel a tug on his heart from Someone above to get himself straight, and soon.

He thinks about talking to her, but isn't sure how to go about it. It's Thursday when he gets home from the hospital and there isn't a lot he can do. Trinity won't let him do anything around the house, so he sits, watches television, and reads. He is pretty much bored out of his mind. By the time Saturday night arrives, he thinks he will lose his mind. Thankfully, she surprises him by inviting Gloria and Katherine over for dinner and she cooks chicken parmesan with a Greek salad. He enjoys the company more than he thought he would since he isn't used to having three women in his house at the same time.

With the house filled with their voices, Sheeba excited by the extra attention, and the aroma of the fine cooking, he has to admit it is one of the best days he has had in a long time. In a way it feels like a holiday. As they eat Sheeba sits near them with her pitiful, begging eyes. They talk about various things that, for once, don't have to do with him getting shot.

"So, have you thought anything about getting your things from Connecticut?" Katherine asks Trinity.

"Yes, it has definitely crossed my mind quite a bit. I'm not sure how I'm going to do it yet, but I don't have much there I really want. Mainly my car, my cameras and photo albums, and my clothes. Most of what I have there I can donate somewhere."

"How long do you think it would take you to do what you have to do?" Gates asks her. "I can take you whenever you want to go."

"And I can go with you if it's okay," Katherine offers. "As long as it's not going to take more than a few days."

"Oh, the drive there and back will take longer than what needs to be done. I need to talk to the landlord and let him know I'm moving out. I'm sure he'll want to know how long it will take to get everything out so he can rent the place, which means Derrick's family will need to get involved. I dread having to talk to any of them, but it will need to be done, I guess."

"God will be with you all the way," Gloria tells her. "Have faith and you'll be okay, even if it doesn't feel like it at the time."

"Thank you, I know He will. I have Him and all of you to get me through whatever happens. I am truly blessed."

Gates watches her expressions as she talks about

something that will probably be painful for her. Through everything she has been through, he knows she has more strength than most men. He listens to her talk to her friends about God, and can't help but admire the beauty that glows from her every pore. Not only is she beautiful on the outside, but more importantly her personality and love for God stands out like nothing he has ever seen before. How can a man hurt her, in any way, shape or form? He doesn't understand it, but he knows he will never harm her. He's too far gone with his feelings for her and will do anything to prove it.

"There's something else I wanted to talk about too, Gloria. I was wondering since you have an extra room if you would be interested in renting it out to me. I'll be looking for a job once I get back from Connecticut, and I already have a bank account. I can pay my rent with no problem."

Gloria laughs out loud. "I've always believed that God steps in when the time is right. It's funny that you ask me now, because I was planning on posting on the church's community board tomorrow that I can use a roommate. Not only because it will help me pay the bills, but I do get lonely sometimes, being by myself."

Trinity beams when she hears Gloria tell them that. "That's great! Yes, God is definitely good! How much are you thinking about renting the room for?"

"Well, I was going to ask for five hundred a month and that includes utilities. Do you think you can handle that much?"

Nodding, Trinity answers, "Yes, that won't be a

problem at all. Even with me not working at the moment I still make money from past jobs I had in other states for certain magazines."

"If you want to you can come over and look at it tomorrow after church, and you can bring your dog with you, too."

Gates and Trinity both laugh at the same time about Sheeba, but she speaks first. "Actually, she's not mine, she's Gates', but the way she is with me you would think she is mine."

Gates speaks up. "I bought her thinking she would be good to have around here, but she doesn't have nearly as much to do with me as she does Trinity. If you want to take her you can. She loves her like a momma. I can get another dog when Trinity moves out if I get too lonely."

"Are you sure?" she asks excitedly.

Grinning, he says "Yes, of course."

Trinity blows him a kiss. "I love you."

Katherine and Gloria "oooh" and "ahhh" over this exchange. They all talk a little more about her moving and having to go to Connecticut, then they clean the kitchen. Trinity finally gives in to Sheeba begging for food and gives her a small treat.

"Did you hear that girl? You will be moving with me and living with Gloria." Sheeba isn't paying her any attention. She's too busy staring at the treat Trinity holds in her hand—something way more important at the moment.

After everything is cleaned up and put away, Katherine and Gloria say goodnight.

"Trinity, I will see you at church tomorrow," Gloria says. "Gates, will you be there too?"

"Yes, I think me being there would be in my best interest. I plan on going."

"Good, I look forward to seeing you both. After, we'll go to my place so Trinity can see the house."

After they leave, Trinity gently hugs Gates, still being careful to not hurt his shoulder. She gives him a gorgeous smile and a kiss. "What did you mean by what you said to Gloria?"

"I've been doing a lot of thinking about getting my life right, like you are doing," he tells her as he looks into her green eyes. "This experience truly opened my eyes and I need to go. I can feel it in my heart that I need to be there."

Trinity smiles at him and buries her face in his chest. She can hear his heartbeat and the sound almost makes her cry. She's certainly grateful that God isn't ready for him quite yet.

"I'm so glad you feel that way. I can't tell you how scared I was that I almost lost you forever."

He holds her with his good arm, his lips burn for hers to touch his, and he stares into her eyes, knowing he could get lost in them forever.

***

Trinity

Sunday morning turns out to be an incredibly gorgeous day. The temperature is warmer than the weather man predicted. Very few clouds touch the blue in the sky and the squirrels invade the back yard once more before winter starts to set in. Trinity wraps herself in her robe and steps out onto the deck to watch Sheeba play, and sits with Gates as they enjoy their first cup of coffee for the day.

"Good morning, beautiful," Gates greets her.

Smiling she replies, "Good morning to you, handsome. How's your shoulder?"

"It's starting to feel better, but it's still tender. I expect that it will be that way for a while, though. The last time I was shot it hurt for a month and the tenderness was there for at least three months."

Trinity's expression saddens. "Is your shoulder still giving you trouble sleeping?"

"Ehhh, not too bad I guess, but it could be better. I doubt I'll get a good night's sleep for another week or so. There are always naps in between though."

"That's very true," she agrees. "I've always loved a good long nap. Have you had any more bad dreams lately?"

Shaking his head he says, "Thankfully, no. Which in a way surprises me, but I'm not complaining."

Sheeba barks at some squirrels and tries to catch one, making them laugh at her. Gates cheers her on as she does her best, but she never gets close enough to any of them.

"I'm nervous," Gates says out of the blue, making her look at him with some concern.

"Why, baby? What are you nervous about?"

"I don't know, maybe nervous is the wrong word. I guess I mean anxious. I think it's because of what the road ahead presents."

"What do you mean? Are you referring to me moving?

He grins at her and assures her it isn't that. "No, I think it's because I know I need to do something that will change my life forever. I guess it's about having faith more than anything else."

Trinity is beginning to get an idea about what he may be talking about. "Are you talking about church and about getting your life straight?"

He nods and looks out at Sheeba, watching her, admiring her pure freedom as he sips his coffee. He looks at Trinity as she lays her soft hand on his arm and lightly squeezes. She can see his eyes becoming misty; she hasn't seen the sensitive side of him like this before. It touches her soul to see it now.

"Would you like to pray about it? God will always comfort you if you let Him."

Without thinking about it he answers, "Yes, I would like that."

Trinity turns in her seat, facing Gates and takes his hands in hers. They close their eyes and she talks to Jesus loud enough for them both to hear.

"Jesus, my Lord and Savior, I know You are right here with us and I thank You for Your grace, love and blessings. I thank You for all that You have done and are doing and will be doing. Right now, though, the man You put in my life confessed to me about You pulling on his heart. He's open to change in his life. He's open to Your love and presence in his life, Lord Jesus, so I ask of You to guide him, to comfort and strengthen him, and give him courage. I know all that You do is good and that You put us in each other's lives for a reason and I thank You. In Your Heavenly name I pray, amen."

She thinks Gates will say amen as well, but instead he begins to speak to Jesus too, still holding her hands. She breathes in and listens, incredibly thankful for their moment together with God.

"Jesus, I know I don't talk to You nearly enough, but that's going to change. A lot of things will change from this moment forward. I have no idea what You have planned for me, but I know it's something good, otherwise I wouldn't still be sitting here with this angel next to me. I want to get to know You, and I want to believe the same way she does so I ask You to give me courage and comfort. I ask if You will open my heart and soul at church today so that whatever the message is it will help me. Thank You, amen."

Trinity and Gates open their eyes as warm, fresh tears slowly run down their cheeks. Trinity is grinning at him and reaches out to hug him. For a moment she forgets about his shoulder, but when a sharp pain hits him he lets her know it.

"Oh, I'm sorry! I'm so sorry!" she exclaims.

"It's okay, no worries." He reaches out his other hand and caresses her cheek then cups her chin within his palm. "I hope you don't mind me saying that you are amazingly beautiful and when I look at you I see nothing less than perfection."

She isn't used to hearing compliments; his words bring forth another smile. "First off, of course I don't mind. A girl needs and wants to be told she's beautiful." She leans in and kisses him. "And secondly, I'm not perfect and I look like a mess. My hair is all over the place and I don't have any make-up on."

He laughs out loud and reminds her that God doesn't make mistakes, so yes in a way she is perfect and in his eyes, she will always be beautiful.

"I love you."

"I love you too," he replies, "but we best get some breakfast and get ready if we are going to be on time."

***

Gates

They get ready and arrive at church as the band plays and the first song is being sung from the hymn book. Trinity is beautiful, wearing her lavender cotton dress with her hair tied up in a bun. Gates feels uncomfortable in his dress slacks and tie, but she says he looks incredible. Both are smiling as they walk in holding their Bibles, her arm wrapped around his. Walking down the middle aisle they see Gloria, and she waves them over to sit with her. It's only the second time Gates has been in church with Trinity, but it is the first time he is there to really hear the message. He's calmer than he thought he would be. As the Pastor walks up to the pulpit, Gates listens intently, ready to hear whatever God wants him to hear.

After he greets everyone, the Pastor talks about a rich man who had all of the luxuries he could have and that he never did without. He ate the finest foods and drank the very best of wine. Servants were at his beck and call and women swarmed around him. The Pastor then talks about a very sick

189

man named Lazarus whose body was covered with sores. He was put outside next to the rich man's gate, wanting only to eat the scraps of food the rich man threw out. Even the dogs come out to lick Lazarus' sores.

Gates sits, leaning forward hearing every word as the Pastor tells of both men dying. Lazarus is carried away by angels and the rich man suffers greatly in torment. The rich man can see Lazarus in the arms of Abraham being comforted while he suffers and cries out for mercy. He begs for Lazarus to dip his finger in water and to cool his tongue so it will ease his pain and misery. But, Father Abraham reminded the rich man when he had wealth, Lazarus had none. Abraham also reminded him when Lazarus suffered at his doorstep and needed help, he would give none. It was too late for the rich man and there won't be any help.

Tears fill Gates' eyes as he listens to the message, and when the Pastor tells of the rich man begging for Lazarus to talk to his brothers so they can be saved, but Abraham said they have Moses and the prophets to talk to. The rich man's brothers will have to learn from them. Gates feels Trinity squeeze his hand and he smiles at her. He looks back to the front of the church and watches the Pastor lead the congregation in a song he hasn't heard in many years—"Just As I Am." The song is meant to invite anyone who wants to change their life up to the front of the church. If they want to ask Jesus Christ to be their Lord and Savior before they have no more chances and end up where the rich man is forever…in torment.

Gates feels a lump in his throat as he fights back burning tears. He feels something, or Someone, pulling on his soul and heart, and he knows exactly Who it is. It is God, beckoning him to walk to the front of the church. To turn his life over to Him. A quarter of the way through the song he lets go of Trinity's hand and stands. He walks to the front of the church with shaking knees and sweating brow, making the best decision of his life. When he gets there he tells the Pastor he's ready, that he needs and wants Jesus to be his Savior, and that he believes. The Pastor kneels with him in front of everyone and prays, leading him through the words that will forever change his life.

"Jesus, I am a sinner and have never lived with You in my life before now, but I want You in my life now. I believe that You died for me on the cross for my sins and I ask that You forgive me for the sins I have done. I ask that You come into my heart and save me. I ask that You be my Lord and Savior Jesus and guide me in my daily life so that I will live for You and not have to burn in hell forever, but live with You in heaven for eternity. I ask that You make me your servant. In Your holy name I pray, amen."

When those words leave his lips Gates immediately feels the change within and he cries tears of joy. Together, he stands with the Pastor and turns and sees Trinity crying with her hands over her mouth. The song ends and the Pastor tells the congregation that they have a new believer in their midst and everyone claps and cheers. Gates knows he has found a new home to worship God and pure joy fills his soul. After the final prayer, everyone welcomes Gates, making him feel like family. Trinity walks up to him, still drying her tears, and wraps her arms around him.

"I can't express how thrilled I am for you! This just became the best day ever!"

Gloria walks up behind her and congratulates Gates on his life-changing decision. When they are finished talking, they follow Gloria to her house to see where Trinity and Sheeba will live.

When they walk in they are grateful to see a kitchen, living room and den that can easily be photographed for a magazine.

"Oh, this is gorgeous!" Trinity says happily.

"So, you like it, then?" Gloria grins and asks her.

They are looking at a large bedroom with a magnificent bay window facing the back yard and an adjoining full bathroom. The bedroom includes a queen-size bed and dark cherry furniture.

"I absolutely love it! Are you sure you only want five hundred a month? I mean this is really nice."

"Oh yeah, that's plenty. To be honest the house is insulated very well so the bills aren't too bad, and I was lucky to get the deal I have on it years ago. Five hundred will be fine."

"I don't know, I mean I would feel better if I give a little more. Why don't I give you six hundred so I won't feel like I'm taking advantage of you?"

Gloria laughs. "Well, that's up to you. You don't have to, but any extra will always be helpful, so if you want to you can."

"It really is a great looking place you have here, Gloria," Gates tells her as he takes in the details.

"Thank you, I'm pretty happy here, the neighbors are very nice, and it's usually a quiet neighborhood."

"So, it's settled then?" Trinity interrupts. "Six hundred a month and you want me as a roommate?"

"A hug will settle the deal."

Laughter follows and Trinity hugs her. She tells Gloria she will go to Connecticut probably within the next week to get her car and other things. When she gets back she'll move in and give Gloria the money then. They agree on everything and can't be happier with how it all turns out.

Chapter Seventeen

Gates walks out of the doctor's office feeling relief rush through him. His doctor informed him that he will be back to normal sooner than expected, and that he is healthy enough to travel. He goes to Connecticut with Katherine and Trinity to get what Trinity needs from her old apartment.

The landlord and Derrick's family are more cooperative and understanding than Trinity thought they would be. She knows she has God to thank for that. Derrick's family takes care of most of what needs to be done because they know she wants to move on with her life. They don't blame her for what happened. With her car and what little she wants to take back with her, she's relieved of the presence that overshadowed her for so long.

They make sure to stop in and see Howard and Mattie while they are there; it's great to see them again. They are saddened by what happened to Trinity's ex-boyfriend, but very happy for her and Gates. Gates rides with Trinity as they follow

Katherine back to Virginia, thankful that the drive isn't horrible. They expected snow, but didn't have to drive through much of it. When they get back to Moneta it is almost midnight, and Katherine agrees to stay with them for the night.

***

Trinity

Trinity walks into the bathroom as Gates is brushing his teeth and she leans into him, feeling the warmth of his body against her.

"I have an idea. Why don't I let Katherine sleep in my bed tonight and I sleep with you? That way we can cuddle and wake up together tomorrow."

Almost choking on the toothpaste, he spits, rinses his mouth, and gapes at her. "Are you sure?" he asks as she smiles at him. He will never, ever get tired of looking into her eyes or being blessed by her smile.

"Well, I think I can control myself if you can. If you don't think you can...I understand," she teases.

Gates laughs at her when she pushes out her bottom lip and tries to pout. He pulls her tighter against him.

"Trust me, it isn't that I don't want you with me; it's just a shock that you suggest it is all. It will be difficult, especially since nothing has happened between us yet."

"I know, but it would be so nice to snuggle and wake up with you tomorrow."

He takes a deep breath and rolls his eyes which

makes her slap his arm. Chuckling, he says, "I agree, that would be really nice."

"I thought you would see it my way," she jokes and walks out of the bathroom to tell Katherine she can sleep in her room. Trinity takes Sheeba out one more time. When they get back inside, Sheeba follows her into Gates' room, looking out of place.

Trinity says, "I think we will have God and Sheeba watching over us to make sure nothing happens."

Together, they pray and voice their gratitude and love for Christ then slide beneath the covers until they are as close together as they can possibly be. With her cheek against his chest, she hears the beating of his heart and for the first time she thinks about how it will be to officially have their hearts beating as one. The idea of spending the rest of her life with Gates pleases her. She is amazed at how quickly things have moved since they first met. She isn't certain how he feels about marriage and she has no plans on scaring him away by bringing it up. She will wait until they are together for a while before hinting at it.

***

Gates

As Gates stares at the ceiling and caresses Trinity's back, he feels like he has never in his life been as in love as he is right now. Here he is in bed, holding a woman he feels is perfection. He truly believes God blessed him with her, and he isn't doing anything to disrespect her. They both made sure to wear something appropriate, and he's totally content holding her and nothing else. That alone surprises him. He knows it would have been different a few years ago. Not that he would ever force himself, but he wouldn't be nearly as respectful with a woman as he is now. He wonders what she's thinking as they hold each other. He wonders what she would think about getting engaged. This is the first time in his life he's had serious thoughts about getting married, and he's glad it never happened before. He knows if it had he wouldn't be holding true beauty in his arms right now. He is truly blessed and he knows it.

Am I ready to settle down and get married? What would it be like to be a married man and maybe have a couple kids? Not so long ago those ideas would have terrified him and he would have run, but not any longer. The idea of spending the rest of his life with Trinity and being a father feels right. It feels like something God wants them to do. Tomorrow he will help her move into her new place with Gloria, and after that he will think of some excuse, without lying, so he can get away for an hour or so to look at engagement rings. And knowing him…buy one. "What are you thinking about?" she asks him. Startled from his thoughts he replies, "You."

"So am I."

"You are thinking about you, too?" he jokes.

"Duh, no dork, I was thinking about you."

"Dork?" he laughs and she raises her head to look at him.

"Yes, my dork."

"Always," he grins. Immediately he knows he will definitely ask her to marry him. To spend the rest of her life with him and raise a family.

***

Trinity

The next morning the weatherman says they may get eight inches of snow later that afternoon. Katherine eats breakfast with them and leaves to go home before the snow starts.

"Congratulations on having your life back and for finding a place so easily. I like Gloria and think everything will be great for you, but I really need to get home."

"Thank you. Thanks for going with us to Connecticut and everything else. I'm so glad we became friends." Trinity hugs her before she leaves.

Katherine hugs her back. Whispering in Trinity's ear, she says, "You have a great guy here. Hang on to him."

"I have every intention of doing just that."

After Katherine leaves, Trinity gets what things she has at Gates' place together and puts them in his car since hers is full already. She has barely enough room left for Sheeba. They drive over to her new residence, stopping by an ATM on the way. Trinity withdraws six hundred dollars to pay her first month's rent.

When they arrive at Gloria's, the house is unoccupied. There is a note on the counter to let them know she's excited about Trinity being there. She will see her later; she has to run to the store before the snow starts to fall. They get everything into her room while Sheeba investigates the entire place—as any curious pet would do. Trinity watches Gates to make sure he doesn't overdo anything and reinjure himself.

"I'm going to love it here," Trinity tells Gates as he holds her.

"Yeah, I think you will, too. I hate to rush off so fast and leave you, but I have to go somewhere before it gets bad outside."

"Oh." Trinity pouts. "Where are you going? You need to get bread and milk, too?" "Ummm, no not really, but I have to get something. It's a secret, but I think you'll like it."

She's suddenly curious and pokes him, asking what it is. "What is it? Come on, tell me."

Laughing, and holding her wrists to keep her from tickling him, he says, "It wouldn't be a secret if I told you. I promise I'll let you in on it very soon, just not right now."

"Oh, okay. If you say so."

"Can I have a kiss before I leave?"

Pursing her lips and looking at the ceiling, she answers, "I don't know…can you?"

Pulling her to him and making her giggle, they kiss and promise to talk later when he gets home.

Trinity watches him drive away, wondering what he has up his sleeve. She thinks about what was on her mind the night before as she snuggled with him. "No…it couldn't be that." She shakes her head, looks at the gathering clouds in the sky, and knows it won't be long before the white stuff starts to fall. She closes the door and begins putting her things in their place.

***

Gates

Gates stands in front of the glass counter and admires all the gorgeous rings as they glitter back through the glass at him. It's like they are talking to him with their own special language. His heart races with the excitement and anticipation coursing through him. He knows she will be happy with any one of them, but he wants to find the perfect one for the perfect woman. It doesn't take long for his gaze to spot the ideal ring. Gates asks the lady behind the counter if he can look at it. She takes it out and hands it to him, telling him more about it.

"She will be a very lucky lady to wear that. It's called the Tiffany Circlet; its shape stands for eternal devotion. It has a brilliant central diamond surrounded with pave` set diamonds to create the perfect circle of white light, and is a shining tribute to love everlasting."

"Not only do you make it sound beautiful, but it truly is as well. How much is it?" he asks, already knowing it will be very expensive. But worth it.

"Today is your lucky day. Normally, that ring would cost five thousand dollars, but we have a sale today so it's going for forty-two hundred. I think you'll agree that's a good deal."

Gates' heart thumps against his chest and for a

second there is a ringing in his ears. Forty-two hundred dollars for one piece of jewelry. He grins at himself because he knows Trinity is worth every penny, and a whole lot more. He also knows he isn't leaving without it. He pulls out his credit card and hands it to the saleslady.

"She will not be disappointed, and congratulations," she says as she takes his card.

"Thank you."

Gates waits for her to complete the sale and thinks about possible disappointment. The only one who might be disappointed will be him if she says no. He will definitely need God's help. The saleslady hands his card back, and the small blue box that holds his future. Gates walks back to his car. Once he's in the driver's seat he closes his eyes, smiles at what he is planning, and thanks Jesus for the courage to do so.

"Lord, Jesus, thank You for blessing me with the courage to buy her this ring and for the ability to doing so. I'm not one hundred percent sure when I'll ask her, but as You know I will need Your help with that. Thank You."

By the time he gets home snow starts to fall from the darkening sky. By the way it's sticking to the ground, it might be a bad one. They are calling for eight inches, but sometimes weathermen are off a little. It might be more.

Gates pulls into his driveway and rushes inside from the cold. He thinks about starting a fire, but that seems romantic and will only make him want Trinity here for the first fire of the season. Instead, he turns the heat to about seventy degrees and takes a shower. It feels weird not seeing Sheeba prancing around. It's going to take a little getting used to, not having either of them here with him.

As he showers, he's again amazed at how fast they have fallen for each other. Because of that and with everything else that has happened, he truly believes she is the one he's always heard was made for him. For him. He smiles when he thinks about that. Once he's settled he calls her, eager to hear her voice again.

"Jeez, I feel like a teenager," he murmurs and grins as he waits for her to answer.

"Hey there," Trinity greets him. "I guess you made it home safely."

"I did, and I miss you already. It doesn't seem the same without you here. The house feels empty."

"I miss you, too."

"Are you excited, though? About being there, I mean."

"Yeah, I am, and Sheeba seems to like it here too. I'm not sure, though, because she keeps walking around being nosy and getting into everything."

Gates laughs. "She's only checking the new place out is all. She'll get used to it. You both will. That's what dogs do."

They talk some more about putting her things away, about the weatherman saying there could be more snow in a couple of days, and how she needs to start looking for a job.

"I guess since I have my laptop back I can put in some applications online if I find something I like. Plus, I can make sure my resume is updated. If not,

I'll have to touch it up some."

"That's a good idea. I'm not sure what I will do tomorrow. I haven't really thought too much about it to be honest."

"You could always come over here and see me."

"Well, yeah, that's a given." They laugh at that.

Trinity ends the call, saying "I'm going to fix something to eat then shower, but I will call you back before I go to bed. Before I leave, though, I was thinking a little while ago that I have never really had a roommate. Not counting Derrick and when I stayed with you. This is a first for me and it'll be a learning experience, but in a good way. I think Gloria and I will be great living together."

"Yeah, you'll get close in no time, honey."

"I miss and love you."

"I miss and love you, too."

He lays his phone on the table and stares at the blank television. He doesn't even want to turn it on. Turning his head, he sees his Bible sitting on the other side of the room and goes to pick it up.

Now is as good a time as any to get into Gods word. Picking up his neglected Bible, he sits back and rests on the couch with a lamp on behind him. Having never seriously gotten into the Word before now he isn't sure where to start.

Opening it before him he lets his heart guide him and decides to read from the book of Revelation. He had always heard that was the most intense book about the coming of Christ and what would happen when He returns. He doesn't know why, but for some reason that feels like the perfect place to begin.

203

Later that evening he talks with Trinity again. They both are in bed, in separate houses, reading to each other from the Bible. He tells her he read from Revelation earlier and she is impressed.

It isn't the same as being at his kitchen table reading together, but it's still special to both of them. They decide to start a regular schedule at night before bed, starting with Matthew and reading the Gospels first, then maybe skipping back to the Old Testament. When they are finished reading for the night, Gates tells her he is thinking about looking online to see what kind of Bible classes he can take. He's interested in learning what he can to help him on his journey.

She also suggests he talk to the pastor, saying he can probably guide him in the right direction.

They say goodnight and after hanging up, individually say their prayers. They don't know what God's plan is, but they are more than willing to keep moving forward together to find out.

***

The next morning the ground is covered with close to a foot of snow. Gates has a hard time getting to Trinity's house, but he has no intention of staying home and away from her. Shortly after his arrival, she talks him into going outside to build a snowman.

"Ohhh, you just wait! I'll get you back for that!" Trinity screams at him as he laughs and ducks when she throws a snowball at him in return, but she misses by several feet. She tries chasing him, but has difficulty, especially with Sheeba jumping around wanting to play at the same time. They got four inches more than what was called for, but they don't mind. They are having a good time anyway. Inside, Gloria is making some hot cocoa as they act like kids. It's a beautiful day for them all.

"The cocoa is ready!" Gloria yells through the small kitchen window. "Please, take off your boots before tramping snow through the kitchen."

"Yes, ma'am," they yell back, laughing like they are talking to their mother. They shake the snow off their boots before removing them and place them inside the foyer. Gates yells and squirms when he suddenly feels a handful of snow slide down the back of his shirt.

"I told you I would get you," Trinity laughs and scurries away to hide behind Gloria.

"Don't get me involved in your games," Gloria tells the two of them. "Drink your cocoa before it gets cold."

Trinity and Gates eye each other with grins on their faces as they sit at the table to enjoy the cocoa. Seconds later, their feet are touching and playing beneath the table. Gloria sees them, but doesn't say a word as she smiles at the evident love each has for the other.

Chapter Eighteen

Trinity

Another week flies by and Trinity feels like things are beginning to feel normal in her life again. It's been years since she felt as good as she has lately. That she isn't afraid or stressed out is tremendously good for her, and having real friends is truly a blessing. She and Gloria are quickly getting close and she's beginning to feel like a part of Gloria's family. The things she is most grateful for are the deep relationships she has with God and Gates. She knows without a doubt she is madly in love with Gates, and every second she is able to spend with him she treasures

During the previous week, Trinity spent some time with Gloria enjoying deep conversations. Some were about Gloria's journey into faith and some about her life beforehand. Trinity shared some precious memories of her past as well, but left out the most painful ones. She would rather they stay behind her.

When she wakes Saturday morning, she is happy to see that most of the snow has melted. She feels she can safely go out and get a few errands done once she gets dressed. First things first…she says her prayers, takes Sheeba out then makes her usual cup of coffee. Sheeba lies on the floor chewing her long-knotted rope as Trinity sips her coffee and watches the news. She doesn't pay too much attention to it, though. She doesn't like all of the negativity. She looks at the clock to see what time it is because she wants to talk to Gates before she gets in the shower and heads out. She decides to take the chance and call anyhow. If he doesn't answer she will leave a message. He answers on the second ring.

"Good morning, beautiful," he greets her with a husky voice.

"Good morning; I guess I woke you."

"Yeah, but it's okay. I need to get up. I didn't go to sleep until late and didn't set my alarm last night."

"Oh, okay. I slept like a baby," she told him.

"Lucky you."

She giggles and asks, "What are your plans for the day?"

"After I do a workout, I plan on getting online and looking for some classes to take. I am really interested in getting deep into the Bible and learning as much as I can. I might even look up the Bible college in Lynchburg and see what they offer."

The fact that he's serious about his faith in Christ excites her and without realizing it her grin covers her entire face. Sheeba gets on the couch with her and Trinity rubs the top of her head as she talks with Gates.

"That's fantastic! I'm very proud of you for doing that. I'm excited for you, too. Let me know what you find."

"I will. If it doesn't take up too much time I'm thinking about putting an ad in the paper for some handyman work, too. I've taken it easy for a few months and I don't need the money, but it wouldn't hurt to be doing something a few days a week."

"Well, you go on with your bad self," she jokes.

"What will you be doing today?"

"Once I get ready I'm going to go to Bedford and put in a resume at a few places, but more specifically at the newspaper. I really want to get back into photography. I should probably look more online, too. I might find something there as far as magazines go. If I'm not gone too long and the roads are safe enough, I might go to Roanoke and do the same. I'm not sure yet on that one, though. I know it's Saturday, but I figure why wait. I don't want to sit around. I want to get out and be productive for a change, then come home and relax with you."

"Please be careful. I know a lot of the snow has melted, but there are probably still some icy patches on the road. It's still pretty cold out, and the side roads won't be as well maintained as the main roads."

"I will, I promise."

"Well, I guess I should get out from beneath these covers if I'm going to get anything done. I'll see you when you get here later, then you can tell me all about your day."

"Yes, I'll definitely do that, and I'll bring pizza so we can eat and I can give you a kiss."

"Now that sounds like a great idea. I love the way you think, and the pizza sounds good too."

She laughs. "Good luck on your search, and I'll talk with you later."

***

It's colder than she thought it would be as she sits shivering in her car, waiting for it to heat up. Trinity thinks she should get the defroster checked because it doesn't seem to be clearing the windshield fast enough. She also decides that the next car she buys will have seat warmers in it. She never has liked the cold, one thing she definitely won't miss about Connecticut. The winters there are horrid.

She forgot that even in the south it can still get bitterly cold. It takes at least five minutes before the heat begins blowing from the vents and brings some relief. She'll have to remember to wait inside next time as it heats up. Maybe her next car will be one she can start without having to go outside. That thought brings a smile to her face.

She listens to an old CD she found among her things as she was unpacking. It takes her down memory lane a bit, before things got bad in her life. She feels things are certainly improving as she drives down the curvy, empty road on her way to Bedford, excited about the day ahead and being productive. She wrote out a list of things to do while she is out, and by the end of the day, she'll be relaxing on the couch with Gates. She might take Sheeba with her, too.

While daydreaming about Gates, she neglects to pay full attention to a curve she approaches and is caught off guard when her tires hit a thick patch of ice. Within a matter of seconds her car careens off the road into a large field on her right, turning over repeatedly, knocking her unconscious and bleeding.

The day isn't close to how she wanted it to be. She hangs upside down from her seatbelt, the tires spinning above, glass from shattered windows covering her, and her own blood trickling down the side of her face as gasoline leaks onto the frozen ground.

She is unaware of everything around her. She doesn't hear the man screaming at her as he gets closer, asking if she is okay, or the man's wife talking to the 911 operator on her cell phone.

***

Gates

Gates glances over at the clock and can see that it's almost four o'clock. He is getting worried about Trinity. It has been close to seven hours since they last talked and he really figures she would be on her way over by now or at least have called him. The pizza is the least of his concerns; though he desires her kiss, he longs to hear her voice even more with every growing moment. Finally, after deciding he

210

can't wait any longer he picks up the phone to call her. He doesn't want to interrupt her in case she got lucky and is in the middle of a job interview or something else important, but feels the need to check on her. He knows the roads are still icy and dangerous. Before he has the chance to push a single button on the phone it vibrates in his hand. Unfortunately, it isn't her.

"Hello."

"Gates, this is Gloria."

"Hey, Gloria."

"I'm sorry to be the one to have to tell you this, but I have some bad news. Trinity was in a terrible accident this morning and she's in the hospital."

His heart immediately clenches with an iron fist and he bolts upright from the sofa. "What? Where? In Bedford or Roanoke? Is she okay?"

"I'm not sure of all the details. The hospital in Bedford just called me and I'm getting ready to go over there now. If you want me to stop and get you I will."

"That's okay, I can't wait. I'll be out of here in seconds. Thank you for letting me know. I'll see you there."

Not realizing it, he hangs up on Gloria. He has his shoes and coat on and is out the door within minutes. He revs up his Jeep and even though he doesn't want to take the time to do it, he has no choice but to scrape the thin sheet of ice that's on the windshield. Part of him is thankful, though, because it reminds him to be careful.

Because it is quickly growing dark, the possibility of hitting ice, and knowing his mind is distracted, it takes him longer to get to the hospital than he anticipated, but eventually he arrives safely. He parks and rushes into the emergency department asking for her and if she has been admitted.

"Are you a family member, sir?" the young blonde nurse with horn-rimmed glasses asks.

"No, but I might as well be. I'm her boyfriend."

"And I'm her roommate," he hears Gloria say as she walks in behind him.

When she steps up beside him they quickly hug and wait to see if they are going to be able to see her. The nurse looks at them with compassion. She can tell from their expressions they are in panic mode and need to be able to see her.

"She was admitted to a room earlier today and normally only family is supposed to be allowed in."

"She's only been living here a few months. She doesn't have family around here. We are all she has and she doesn't know it yet, but I'm going to ask her to marry me," Gates says. Gloria looks at him in surprise and rubs his back, but doesn't say anything. When the nurse sees the desperation in their eyes she sighs, purses her lips, and tells them what little she can.

"I understand your situation and I'm sorry. I will tell you that she's going to be okay, although she was banged up pretty bad."

"Can you tell me anything? How bad is she hurt?" Gates asks.

"When she came in she was unconscious. She has a concussion, and her left leg is broken below the knee. She has been put on some pain medicine to help her cope with it. You two go ahead. She's in room number four zero four."

"Thank you," they tell her as they quickly turn to find the elevator.

Together they walk into Trinity's room, holding their breaths and with nerves about to go over the edge. She's asleep, probably from the drugs they administered, so they sit by her bed waiting and hoping. They see her leg is in a cast and she has stitches on the side of her head. Hopefully, there won't be a scar.

Gates is fidgety and his heart is pounding. He prays and is thankful she isn't hurt more than she is. For some reason, he thinks about when she gets out if she will say yes to marrying him. Seeing her lying there and knowing she could have died makes him decide to ask her sooner than he planned. If he had thought to grab the ring he could have asked her here at the hospital when she wakes up. He knows he will have to go home later to get some things and come back, so he will have to remember to get it then.

Gates and Gloria sit and wait as patiently as they can and the time seems to drag like they have never known it to before. Finally, after what feels like forever, Trinity moans and moves her head slightly. Gates bolts out of his chair and gently takes her hand in his, speaking softly to her. "Trinity…sweetheart, it's Gates."

Trinity opens her eyes and even though she's dazed from the effects of the drugs, trauma, and confusion, she knows who is talking to her, who is holding her hand, and she smiles weakly.

"Hey," she mumbles, "I'm so sorry." As soon as

she speaks, tears fill her eyes and leave tracks down her cheeks.

"Sorry for what, honey?" he asks. He softly caresses her cheek and wiping away her tears. "For scaring you."

His heart twists in his chest as he watches the woman he almost lost cry in front of him. She is worried about what he thinks, not what happened to herself. He leans over her and kisses the tip of her nose. "I'm okay because I know you will be. I love you."

"I love you, too," she replies and reaches up to touch his stubble. "You didn't shave today." A burst of laughter comes from Gates and Gloria, and Trinity realizes Gloria is there too. Gloria stands next to her and caresses her arm, letting her know that everything will be okay.

"I have to admit this scared the dickens out of me, too, but I'm glad you are okay. When you get home I'll take care of you like you're my daughter."

Gates immediately speaks up, saying, "Ummm, please forgive me if I step on any toes here, but I have every intention of taking care of her at my place."

Grinning at him, Gloria replies, "Dear, I understand that you are madly in love with her and you are so sweet, but do you plan on helping her in and out of the bathtub, too?"

He looks at her, then to Trinity with a sheepish look of confusion, unsure how to respond. They both laugh at him, causing Trinity to cringe from the pain in her head. Obviously, the pain medicine is wearing off.

"I think it might be a good idea that I stay home for a little while sweetie, but thank you for wanting to take care of me. I would love it if you could spend as much time with me as you can, though."

"You can be sure that I will, and I will try not to be in the way too much."

"I'm sure you will be in the way plenty, but I'll overlook it," Gloria responds jokingly.

The nurse comes in when she hears them talking and asks Trinity how she's feeling.

"I hurt a lot, but I don't want any pain medicine that will make me groggy. I'm also very thirsty. Could I please have some water?"

"I'll be right back with that water and something for your pain," the nurse tells her and walks out.

"Do you have any idea how long you'll have to stay?" Gates asks after the nurse leaves.

"I'm not sure, but probably a day or so I would imagine."

"Well, in that case I guess it's my turn to go and pack a few things and stay here with you. But seriously—we have to stop meeting this way," Gates tells her, trying to throw in a little humor.

Gloria looks at him sideways and Trinity finds it funny, but tries not to laugh so her head won't hurt.

"I have to say, this is my first—and I pray to Jesus the only—concussion that I will ever have," Trinity tells them as she grimaces and tries to sit up. Gates and Gloria help, telling her to move slowly.

The nurse arrives with her water and pain medicine. "Do you need anything else, honey?"

"No, thank you."

When the nurse leaves, Gloria says "I'm going to

leave the two of you alone, go home to make sure Sheeba is okay, and straighten up a little. If you need anything let me know, sweetie." She kisses Trinity on her forehead. "I'll be praying for you."

"Thank you, I really appreciate it. Give Sheeba some sugar for me."

Once Gloria leaves, Gates feels his emotions begin to surface. While Gloria was with them he was able to control them, but now he's looking at the woman he intends to spend the rest of his life with lying in a hospital bed. It's a view he never wishes to see again.

"Are you okay?" Trinity asks him when she sees his expression change.

He nods, takes a breath before responding, and closes his eyes. Re-opening them he says, "Within the past month we almost lost each other. Not long before that we first met. I can't even begin to explain how God works, but I'm trying my best to. I love you, Trinity. I knew that before today, but seeing you hurt has made it more real for me. I don't know if I'm making sense or not, but I hope I am. I know when Gloria called and told me you had been in an accident I thought I was going to have a heart attack."

As her fingers lace within his, her lips tremble. She takes a ragged breath and tries to speak but isn't able to for a moment. When she does it comes out in sporadic bursts. "I love you, too. I truly…believe that God made you…for me."

She stops for a moment and grips his hand tightly. With her other hand she wipes her tears; he sits and waits patiently. He knows she has more to say and isn't going to interrupt.

"You mean the world to me, Gates," she's able to blurt out. "I wish I wasn't in here right now; I would love to just lie down with you and cuddle."

"We will as soon as you get home, I promise." He mentally kicks himself again for not thinking about bringing her ring. Obviously, it isn't meant to happen right now, but he will ask her soon. Maybe after she gets a little better he will do it in a romantic way that she will never forget. He will need to rack his brains to think of something great for her.

Chapter Nineteen

Trinity

After being in the hospital for two days, the doctor informs Trinity that she can go home. She can't be more thrilled by the news. After the last two days in an uncomfortable hospital bed and very little sleep, she's more than ready to leave. Her head still hurts; apparently a concussion isn't something that goes away easily.

She also finds out that getting in and out of Gates' Jeep isn't an easy task with a cast on her leg, but they manage. With some effort on both their parts, she slowly slides onto the back seat. Once he has Trinity home, getting her out of the Jeep and into the house is much more difficult.

Sheeba wants her undivided attention and won't be satisfied until she gets some loving from Trinity. Having to hold her close so she won't hurt her leg, Trinity realizes that she missed the spoiled dog as much as Sheeba missed her.

"Oh, my big baby! I missed you, too!" Trinity rubs her and lets the dog lick her face for a minute with the sounds only a happy dog can make. She has to admit it feels great to not only be home, but to be shown so much love from her fur baby. "Okay...okay girl, that's enough. I know you missed me, but I can't take any more of you licking me."

"Do you want or need anything?" Gloria asks her.

Trinity sees Gloria standing by the doorway of the kitchen with her hands on her hips and her face full of love and compassion. She can't help but imagine her as anything more than a motherly woman and a dear friend. She loves her. "No, I'm okay, but thank you. I don't want you to think you have to baby me, Gloria, but I will appreciate any help you insist on giving me."

"You are welcome, and of course I am going to help. That's what friends do. I'm sure you would do the same for me."

Trinity nods her head in agreement.

"I know one thing I look forward to," she says as she tries to get comfortable on the couch.

"What's that?" Gates asks her.

"I can't wait to get to church! I want to go tomorrow night to the Wednesday night Bible study. I need to hear more of God's Word. I wouldn't be here right now if it wasn't for Him."

Gloria and Gates both agree they need the same, so they all make plans to eat a hearty meal tomorrow evening then go to church.

In the meantime, Trinity gets spoiled more than

the dog. Even though she tries to act as if she doesn't want or need the special attention, her resistance comes across feebly. They all know she relishes in it.

***

"You okay, do you need some help?" Gates asks Trinity as she attempts to slither her way out of the jeep. Trinity is stubborn and determined to do it alone.

"Nope, I got it. Thanks anyway, honey. I have to get used to this since I will be doing it for the next six weeks at least."

Together they slowly make their way to the front door of the church. Gates is by her side, holding both Bibles in one hand and her elbow in the other while she uses crutches to help her walk. When they finally make it indoors and out of the frigid cold, she is bombarded by friends with questions and offers of help.

They make their way to the front so Trinity can stretch her leg out. She is glad to finally sit down when she gets to the pew.

"I'll be glad to get used to these things. My armpits are already sore," she complains.

"Hopefully, you won't have to use them as long as you think," Gates responds, sitting down beside her.

Once the congregation settles, the choir begins singing. To Trinity, it doesn't matter what the song is; every note and word touches her heart. She tries to sing with them, but her emotions make it difficult. She loves being in church and hearing songs of praise; they make her feel at peace with everything that's happened in her life.

The Pastor opens his sermon with prayer before beginning his message. He includes thanks that Trinity made it home alive and asks for a rapid recovery. He talks about miracles; it doesn't seem as if he looks at his Bible often, but speaks more from his heart.

"God spoke to me last night as I sat home and struggled with a topic to preach on today," he begins. "It's amazing how once in a while the message is hard for me to find, because I want to bring you His Word to the best of my ability, but I also have to stop and remember that I'm using my will and not His. I have to tell myself that I need to get out of His way and let Him do the talking. So, today He wants me to tell you about miracles. It's almost ironic that this evening we have one sitting in the front row. Welcome home, Trinity."

The Pastor's words touch her heart and she smiles back at him as he continues with his message. "Sometimes, in our chaotic society we are so driven by success, by everyday life, by the stress that we put on ourselves and even happy times, that our hearts, our souls and eyes are blind to the miracles that go on all around us. It's unfortunate, and sad, that there is plenty of evil out there we all see or hear about in the news. Because of the nature of news media, negativity is what we hear about the most. We don't hear about the good things that happen nearly enough, but there is a lot of that, too."

"The Bible mentions miracles happening every day. Jesus performed great miracles from healing the blind, the sick, feeding thousands of people that surrounded Him with two loaves of bread and five fish. He even raised the dead, but many didn't believe He was the Son of God. Today, other miracles happen right in front of our eyes. Yes, technology has provided many miracles, but let's not forget where the technology came from. Where the knowledge came from and the ability to do these things came from. They all came from God. How about the birth of a child? Isn't that a miracle? What about the overdose of an addict or a suicide attempt and that poor soul survives, gets the help they need, and betters their life? Those are miracles too."

"But I want to get deeper into what God wants me to tell you tonight. He wants me to talk about your souls. I hope and pray that every one of you are truly right with God. Not just thinking you are, but knowing that you are. One of the biggest miracles in our world today is humbling yourself and turning your life over to Jesus Christ and living a Christian life. The temptations out there are tremendous. We all hear about and some of us may know from experience the power of the love of money, lust, adultery, anger, gambling, addiction, and so on. But to be able to turn from any or all of those things and live for Jesus Christ is a true miracle. It isn't always an easy decision for someone to give up their own will and follow Christ. We must remember the gifts He has for us abound and are waiting for us all…"

Everyone in the room sits and watches the Pastor

walk back and forth in front of and around the pulpit as he talks. They wear expressions that range from belief to guilt, shame to fear. By the time the pastor finishes with the message and the invitation music begins, at least ten people walk up and kneel down, taking a step toward repentance or heavenly eternity. Tears are shed and hugs are given when the song ends.

The church is full of the Holy Spirit and Trinity and Gates both can feel it within them. She only wishes she could jump around and dance. She's so full of happiness for everyone who accepted Jesus into their lives and that she is there to see them do it. On the way home it's all she can talk about.

***

Once they are inside and sitting on the sofa Gloria asks if they are hungry. They both say they can eat something so she fixes a snack for them before Gates has to leave.

"I wish you could stay, honey," Trinity pouts.

Grinning, Gates replies, "You always look so darn cute when you do that."

"Thank you," she replies with a smile and kiss.

"I would love to stay, but I doubt it would look good. I should get home anyhow. I have something I need to plan."

"Yeah, what's that?"

"I can't tell you. It's a secret."

She rolls her eyes and says, "Oh, no, here you go again with the secrets. You never told me what the other one was. I thought we aren't supposed to keep

223

secrets from each other. Come on...tell me. Please!"

Laughing at her, "I can't and trust me, both of them are part of the same thing. You'll love what they are. I promise you will know very soon."

"I certainly hope so!" she huffs.

After their snack, Gloria tells them good night. Gates takes Sheeba out for a few minutes then gives Trinity a kiss she'll not forget anytime soon.

"I love you, baby," she tells him as she stands on one leg, leaning into his arms.

"I love you too, even if you are a cripple right now."

"Hey!" she exclaims and slaps his arm.

They laugh, kiss again then she watches through the door window as he drives away. She longs for the day when they can share the same bed, but it can't happen unless a miracle happens. Sort of like what the Pastor talked about earlier.

***

Over the next few weeks Trinity gets more used to the crutches. The hardest part is not tripping over her dog. Since she isn't able to drive at the moment, she spends a large portion of her time reading, looking online for jobs, girl time with Gloria and Katherine, and trying to get Gates to tell her what the secrets are. He doesn't give in and her friends all try to change the subject when she brings it up. She is suspicious of them being in on it, and Gates seems to be enjoying her torture.

It snows several more times and she badly wants

to go outside and play in it, but she's scared of slipping and hurting herself again. When she spends time with Gates, they enjoy reading from the Bible and watching movies. Sometimes she stays at his house, but if temptation is too strong she sleeps in the other room with Sheeba. It isn't easy, but they both want to do the right thing.

He talks to her about starting classes soon in Lynchburg. He decided to attend the university there and become a Pastor. When he breaks the news to her, she is thrilled.

"Is that one of the surprises you have been holding out on?" she asks with pure excitement.

"Uhhh, no, I'm sorry, but it's a great one though isn't it?"

"It is, yes, and I am very happy about it, and proud of you. But seriously, you are driving me mad!"

"Okay, I'm sorry, but I still can't tell you. I will let you in on this much. What I am planning will happen this weekend."

"Really?" she exclaims. "That's all you will give me? That's like…two more days from now."

"I know, but I have to have it all worked out first. Trust me, okay."

"It best be worth the wait mister," she warns and pokes him playfully in the chest.

I hope it is too. "It will be," he tells her.

***

Those two days play havoc on Trinity. She can't wait to find out what Gates has planned for her. She

225

still doesn't think it will be anything as extravagant as a proposal, so all sorts of ideas go through her mind. When Saturday finally rolls around, all he will tell her is to wear her prettiest dress and that he will pick her up at six o'clock. That's it; part of her is irritated with him over it all. "I can't believe he's torturing me this way," she mumbles to herself as she finishes getting ready. Her nerves are on edge; she is excited and anxious to finally know what's going on.

He arrives to pick her up a few minutes before six o'clock, and like any other woman he's ever been with, he is made to wait. As he sits on the couch, he talks to God again asking for the help he will need.

"God, I truly believe this is what You want for her and me so I don't know why I'm so nervous, but please help me do what I need to do. Please give me courage and guidance to ask Trinity to be my wife. I love her and need Your help on this since I know You put us together. In Your name I pray, amen."

Gates fidgets, and Sheeba watches him intently as if she knows exactly what he has planned for her human. Finally, Trinity comes out of her room and she is absolutely stunning.

"Wow!" he exclaims profoundly as he admires the perfection before him. She's wearing a knee length purple dress that hangs perfectly on her petite form. Her hair is shaped in a bob cut that encircles her face so it seems to glow as if under a stage light. Her eyes light up the room and his heart feels like it will burst from his chest.

Smiling at him and appreciating the single but

approving word, Trinity replies, "You look rather handsome yourself." She hobbles over to him and plants her warm soft lips on his. "I give you my stamp of approval."

"You arc incredibly gorgeous. I mean you always are, but…wow. Can I stand here and admire you for a while?" he asks, making her giggle with delight at his charm.

"Any other time if you said that to me I might let you. However, you have had me hanging from a thread long enough with your secrets and I'm ready to know what you have up your sleeve, so no—we have to go. Of course, if you want you can admire me while we are out."

"Oh trust me, I will."

The smile on her face is beautiful, but the one in her heart is even more so and out shines it by a mile. Thirty minutes later, Gates parks the car in the lot of the church and she looks at him, confused.

"Are we stopping here for some reason before you take me to dinner?" she asks.

Grinning, he takes her hand in his. "Trust me on this."

She smiles and tries to keep quiet while her heart thumps hard within her chest. She doesn't know what's going on, but she has a feeling this will be an incredible evening. When they walk into the basement of the church, where the dinners and certain church events take place, Trinity gasps at what she sees. Her hand covers her mouth as she stands in shock at the setup that's laid out in front of them. The room is dimly lit with a single table set up in the middle. Most of the lighting is provided by candles and soft romantic music plays over the speakers. What surprises her most are the two people who are standing, waiting to serve them, dressed as if they work at a fine restaurant.

"Howard? Mattie?" she asks and looks at Gates. "What's happening here?"

Grinning, Gates tenderly touches her elbow and leads her to the table. When she gets to it Howard and Mattie hug her and tell her how incredible she looks.

"It's so good to see you both!" she cries. "Why are you here?"

"We are playing our part so we can't talk right now," Mattie replies with a mischievous grin.

Howard pulls out her chair for her. "For you, madam."

Trinity is flabbergasted and sits at the finely laid out table.

Gates simply says, "Just go with the flow, honey."

He kisses her gently, tells her he loves her, then sits across the table from her. She takes in the roses that sit in the middle of the table as a tear escapes her eye. Also in front of her is fancy china and silverware wrapped in napkins and wine glasses. Two tall candles with dancing flames are almost hypnotizing, but when her eyes meet his, her heart flutters wildly for him. Never before in her entire life has anyone done something like this for her. She's speechless.

"Would you like something to drink, ma'am?" Howard asks and hands her a handwritten menu. She opens it and can't help but giggle when she sees the three selections Gates had written for her…red or white apple cider or ginger ale. She decides to play along with the act because not only does she think it's very cute and touching, but she finds the entire situation incredibly romantic.

"Hmmm, the choices are so good. Let me see," she pauses and places a finger to her lips, feigning thought. "I think I will have the red cider, please."

She raises her eyes again to meet Gates and smiles with so much love she thinks she is going to burst at the seams.

"And you, sir?" Howard asks after he fills Trinity's glass.

"I'll have the white cider, please." Mattie gladly fills his glass and when they both stand back, Trinity sees another surprise walking toward them. Katherine and Gloria walk from the kitchen, both holding trays with appetizers. When Trinity speaks to them, they act the part they are given as well. She feels like she is in a dream with all of the best people in her life.

"I'm truly loving the special attention, but can you please talk to me like normal so I will think it's not just a dream."

Gates softly laughs. "Okay, no more acting, just be yourself."

Katherine, Gloria, and Mattie all hug her again and begin chatting away, but stop when Trinity starts asking questions. All four of them leave, smiling, and walk into the kitchen. Gates and Trinity are alone, Trinity more confused than ever.

"Do you like your appetizer? It's chicken corn chowder. You should eat it before it gets cold,"

Gates suggests, trying to play coy.

Trinity stares at him, definitely not thinking about the chowder, but makes herself swallow a few spoonfuls of it so he will be satisfied. She's doing her best to stay calm, but curiosity is killing her and she starts getting antsy. Gates pulls out a piece of paper with something he says he wrote the night before. She sits with her chin resting in her palm and takes in his handsome face as he clears his throat and begins to read.

"The beauty of a rose is immaculate as it opens its petals for all the world to see. The sunrise always begins a new day. But when my eyes meet yours and I'm in your presence, no other beauty can stand before you. No other flower, song or act can be next to you without knowing they can't measure up because when God made you, He created the definition of perfect beauty."

His heartfelt words are like no other she's ever heard before, and even more precious because he wrote them for her. Before she has the chance to comment, Gates stands and takes her hand within his.

"May I have this dance?"

Suddenly, a song she isn't familiar with begins playing and as she listens to the words, she knows it's perfect for them both. Slowly, within his arms, she dances as best she can and stares up into his eyes as the words to "The Keeper of the Stars" play in her mind. She didn't think it was possible to have moments like this in her life, but God is definitely blessing her right now. Her lips tremble and tears flow from her green eyes. Gates wipes her tears and kisses her when the song is finished playing.

"I love you, Trinity."

Gasping for air, she replies, "I love you, too."

Pulling back slightly and like a perfect gentleman, he lowers himself to one knee. Trinity is suddenly faced with the reality that Gates is proposing to her. She struggles to breathe as her tears continue to flow and her knees feel like butter. She thinks she is going to faint when he pulls out the little blue box from his jacket pocket and says the words she wasn't sure she would ever hear.

"Trinity, I know this may be fast, because we have only been in each other's lives a few months, but I have no doubt in my soul that God wants this. I also have no doubt that you are the woman I want to spend the rest of my life with, through everything that comes our way. Will you please give me that honor? Will you be my wife?"

Trinity can see the love and hope in his eyes and at the same time she hears her friends in the kitchen crying. She doesn't have to be asked twice nor does she have to think about his question. She knows she wants the same thing he does. With an exasperated breath, because speaking is near impossible, she simply nods and whispers, "Yes."

Grinning from ear to ear, Gates slides the most gorgeous ring she has ever seen onto her finger. Her friends cry out in joy for them both and she hugs the man God put in her life. They kiss and another song begins playing, but she barely hears it. What she hears is the beating of their hearts. They hold on tight as they dance slowly, careful not to put too much pressure on her bad leg. When the dance is over he helps her to the table so she can rest her leg, and everyone comes from the kitchen to congratulate them.

Afterward, Gates gets up and helps Howard carry over another table and they all have dinner together, making the night even more special. Trinity is thrilled everyone she loves is there for their glorious moment, talking loudly and laughing. The blessings God has given them are amazing and the two of them couldn't be happier.

Epilogue

In the summer…

The sun rises slowly as Trinity sips her coffee and watches the waves meet the sand from the patio of their suite. Seagulls are picking at the sand in search of something to eat. Trinity quietly praises her Lord and Savior for not only the incredible view, but for also waking up this morning. The first morning on their honeymoon. They waited a few months after getting married for warmer weather so they could be where they are now.

"Good morning, my ravishing wife."

She grins and replies as he slides his hands around her waist from behind. "Good morning my amazing and handsome husband."

She giggles as he kisses the nape of her neck and rests back against him. She is still amazed at how her life turned out. Here she is, recently married and madly in love. There no more fear or danger in her life; only God, a man who treasures her, her career, the best of friends, and a new life growing within. She rubs her stomach and wonders when the best time would be to tell Gates, and realizes all of her dreams have come true. For the next two weeks they will be staying in Myrtle Beach and resting, playing and enjoying each other as much as possible. God is good. God is love, and He has surely graced them with His love.

The End

Acknowledgements

First, I want to acknowledge Limitless Publishing for giving me the opportunity of being a part of their family and for believing in my work. Thank you for giving me a chance.

Thank you to J.L. Joyal, my Personal Assistant. With her expertise, I'm able to reach further with marketing, able to make new connections and have a better opportunity to reach my goals. Thank you, J.L Joyal for all your hard work and patience with my bugging you daily.

Thank you to Heather L. Whitehead for doing an incredible job at editing my novel. Thank you for being patient, for your advice and for helping me shape this incredible story into what it is now.

Thank you to all my readers for being patient with me for getting another story out to you. Without having all of you in my life, this would be a drearier process. You all help keep me strong and pushing forward in one of the things I love to do most.

God. Without You I would be nothing. I have absolutely no doubt of this. You have forever been with me and never once gave up on me. I'm still alive today because of You. Literally.

Last but certainly not least, the program and angels that helped shape me into the person I am today. The twelve steps are the key and to everyone within the fellowship that has loved me. For all the angels that have prayed for me and supported me. Much love from my heart to yours.

About the Author

Jamie Lynn Boothe is from the south and will always be a southerner at heart. He currently lives in Connecticut. Jamie loves to write stories that will touch someones heart and soul to the depths and at the same time have them sitting on the edge of their seat. He is currently with Limitless Publishing and is excited about what the future holds. Along with writing he also enjoys reading, art, music, movies, cats, naps on occasion, coffee and time with friends and watching sports. His favorite teams are the Dallas Cowboys and New York Yankees.

Facebook:
http://www.facebook.com/Author-Jamie-Lynn-Boothe-114312728740616/?fref=ts

Twitter:
http://www.twitter.com/boop1967

Goodreads:
http://www.goodreads.com/author/dashboard